SARANORMAL

Yesterday and Today

by Phoebe Rivers

SIMON SPOTLIGHT
New York   London   Toronto   Sydney   New Delhi

SIMON SPOTLIGHT
An imprint of Simon & Schuster Children's Publishing Division
1230 Avenue of the Americas, New York, New York 10020
Copyright © 2013 by Simon & Schuster, Inc. All rights reserved, including the right of reproduction in whole or in part in any form. SIMON SPOTLIGHT and colophon are registered trademarks of Simon & Schuster, Inc. For information about special discounts for bulk purchases, please contact Simon & Schuster Special Sales at 1-866-506-1949 or business@simonandschuster.com.
Text by Sarah Albee
Manufactured in the United States of America 1113 FFG
First Edition   10 9 8 7 6 5 4 3 2 1
ISBN 978-1-4424-8961-5 (pbk)
ISBN 978-1-4424-8962-2 (hc)
ISBN 978-1-4424-8963-9 (eBook)
Library of Congress Catalog Card Number 2013935643

Chapter 1

Alone at last.

Upstairs in my room, I sat on the floor next to my bed. My hands shook a little as I stared down at the diary. My mother's diary. My mother, who I had never met because she died giving birth to me. Now I held in my hands the diary she kept when she was my age. I was finally going to "meet" her . . . at least, sort of.

Earlier in the day, my best friend, Lily, and I had found the diary hidden in a secret closet in a room I usually refer to as "the blue bedroom" because of the blue walls in there. But now Lily had gone home. She'd known without me having to tell her that I wanted to be alone with my mom's diary. I shared just about everything with Lily, but this was different.

I set it down gently in my lap. Brushed it lightly with my fingertips. Took a deep breath.

"Whatcha got there?" demanded a loud voice in my doorway.

I whirled around to see who it was. Could it be my mother?

It *was* a spirit. But not my mother's.

Perhaps I should explain. I can see spirits. People who have died. I've been able to see them for as long as I can remember. The house I live in—the old Victorian house in Stellamar, New Jersey, which belonged to my great-grandmother, Lady Azura—is filled with spirits. My dad and I had moved here two summers ago. At first I didn't know that Lady Azura was my great-grandmother. I'd just thought she was some kooky lady who told fortunes and read tea leaves. She was one of several secrets that had been kept from me for a long time. But I'd grown to love Lady Azura, and by the time I found out she was my great-grandmother, I was thrilled about it.

The spirit standing in my doorway wasn't one I was familiar with. Not one of our regulars, as I had come to think of them. We had several that inhabited the house, and I knew them all. This was an older woman. She had a lot of makeup on, and her hair was all done up like she'd just stepped out of the salon.

I slipped the diary off my lap and nudged it under my bed. Then I stood up and walked over to her.

"Can I help you with something?" I asked, trying to be polite when in reality I was really annoyed by the interruption.

She wandered into my room, checking out my stuff. I bristled as her semitransparent hands touched my things.

"Don't suppose so." She shrugged, examining the photo of my mom on my bedside table. "I was just bored. Name's Shirley. My son, Harry, and his wife are downstairs. They're trying to get me to show up and tell them where I hid my will. I think that's all they care about. And I'll tell them. But in my own sweet time." She laughed mischievously. "It's much more interesting up here."

That explained it, then. My great-grandmother was a fortune-teller. She could conjure spirits. People flocked here for her services.

Lady Azura must be holding a séance with clients downstairs. She must have summoned this spirit for them. I had to get rid of her. Politely, of course.

"Thanks so much for dropping in," I said. "I am sure Harry and his wife can't wait for you to appear to them, though."

"Pah!" she said, waving her hand. "I doubt it. He's a good boy, my Harry. Not sure what he was thinking marrying That Girl, but then, he didn't exactly consult me before he popped the question." Her voice got lower as she started fiddling with my camera. I think maybe she was getting a little emotional. "I did notice that his wife was wearing my butterfly pin. It's an old thing, probably not worth very much anymore. I guess Harry gave it to her after I died. I heard her tell the fortune-teller that it belonged to me and how happy she was to have it. It sort of seemed like she meant it . . . but I think she must think it's valuable and that's why she likes it."

"Actually, I don't think that's true. I can sense that Harry and his wife want you to show yourself. I think they really miss you." To be honest, I wasn't getting much of a vibe from downstairs at all, but I was still pretty sure that what I said was true. And she seemed pleased to hear it. I had learned from Lady Azura that spirits really aren't all that different from the living. They hold grudges and make mistakes just like people do. Sometimes they just need to be set on the right track. "I sense that they're waiting for you, Shirley, and that you must be very important to both of them or else they wouldn't be here."

She stood up, tugging at her dress and patting her hair. "You can sense all that? Do you have the gift, like the lady downstairs?"

"Well, I am her great-granddaughter," I replied. Even I could hear the pride in my voice when I said it.

Shirley regarded me carefully for a moment or two, as if she was trying to make up her mind about me. "All right, then," she said finally. "I shall go join them." And she shimmered into nothingness.

I waited a minute more. I didn't want to be interrupted again. But my room was quiet. I sat down and pulled the diary out from under my bed.

It was light blue, with a puffy kind of cover, sort of like a photo album. Slightly scuffed in places. The word DIARY, embossed in gold lettering, was the only thing on the cover. The corners were bent in a little, as though it had been dropped once or twice.

I took a few deep breaths and tried to calm my racing nerves. This was my first real glimpse into my mother's life, her world. I'd been so eager to meet her, but her spirit hadn't shown itself to me. I'd found out about the diary from another spirit, that of an old sailor named Duggan. Duggan was one of our regulars, and when he was here, he was usually in the blue bedroom. He'd told me about the diary. And then I'd dreamed about where it was hidden. Only Lily and I knew about the diary. I hadn't told my dad or Lady Azura about it. Yet. For now, I wanted it to be my secret. Something I shared with my mother. Just the two of us.

With a trembling hand, I opened to the first page.

Girlish handwriting. Purple ink. Fat, loopy letters. The first entry was dated August 7, 1984.

She would have just turned twelve. The age I was when I first moved to Stellamar. She'd probably received the diary for her twelfth birthday.

A thought struck me. What if she only wrote in the diary for a few days or weeks and then got bored and forgot all about it? That would be really disappointing. But then again, I guessed a small glimpse into my mom's life was better than nothing.

I fanned the pages. There was a lot of writing. She'd stuck with it. The entries came to a stop about two-thirds of the way through the book. Some days had short entries, just a sentence or two. Other days went several pages, the writing growing more urgent and slanted, as though she'd written while upset or excited. I resisted the urge to read these more interesting-looking entries. I'd start from the beginning and read it all in order. I turned back to the first page.

And then my phone vibrated, telling me I had a text.

In exasperation, I pulled my phone from my back pocket. I was going to shut it off, something I almost never ever did, but I didn't want to be interrupted. Then I noticed who the text was from: Lily.

SORRY. I KNOW YOU'RE BUSY WITH YOU KNOW WHAT. BUT PLEASE CALL ME ASAP. IT'S MUCHO IMPORTANT!

I quickly texted back.

OK. WILL CALL SOON.

Then I turned off my phone.

I looked down at the diary. I couldn't wait to meet

her. My mom. Natalie, as she was known to everyone else.

I read the first line . . .

Dear Diary,

. . . and then everything got a little blurry and I was plunged into a vision.

Chapter 2

A girl. About twelve.

She looked exactly as she had looked in my dream. But this vision was much more real than a dream. I felt like I could reach out and touch her.

Her long blond hair was pushed back with a wide headband. She sat on a bed cross-legged, her narrow shoulders hunched as she scribbled away in a blue book. The diary.

This girl was my mother.

I stared at her, taking huge gulps of breath, like I was trying to breathe her in. Study her. Memorize every detail. Long, thick lashes. A sprinkle of freckles across the bridge of her nose. Long, skinny arms and legs. She looked like me. Or I guess I should say, I looked like her.

She was wearing an oversize red shirt that fell off

one shoulder, a pink tank peeking out at the top. Her denim cutoff shorts were rolled up at the bottom. I think her clothes would have been considered stylish back in the 1980s.

The clock on the mantelpiece ticked loudly. She was completely absorbed in her writing.

It was definitely summer. Somewhere in the distance, I could hear the drone of a lawn mower. I darted a look around. I was in the blue bedroom, where Lily and I had found the diary. This was the room my mom used to stay in when she visited Lady Azura. On the dresser was a huge old-fashioned boom box, the kind people used to lug around, blasting music. Clothes were flung across open drawers, draped over chairs, lying in crumpled heaps on the floor. I smiled. I'd learned something I hadn't known before. My mom was kind of messy!

As she continued to write, I moved over to the desk near the window. There were drawings strewn around on it. Charcoal and pastel renderings of the view outside. A bird on a branch. The ocean at sunrise. They were good. Duggan had told me she was an artist. Of course, I knew she had grown up to become a photographer, but it was cool learning that she was into different kinds of art. Just like me.

There was a knock at the door, and then the person just barged in without waiting for my mom to say whether it was okay to come in.

The girl who entered looked to be about my mom's age. She was really small, like my friend Avery. I wondered if she was a gymnast like Avery was. She was dressed similarly to my mom—a baggy T-shirt over a tank, baggy denim shorts with the rolled-up bottoms, and clompy wood-soled sandals with a red leather strap across the top. Her hair was long, curly, pushed back with two combs. On her lips she wore frosty pink lipstick that I thought looked pretty silly but I'm guessing was considered cool back then.

"You ready to rock 'n' roll, Nat?" asked the girl. "My mom just dropped me off and is running to the drugstore. She'll be back to take us to the mall in about fifteen minutes."

"Almost ready," my mom replied, moving to the dresser. She uncapped a fat tube of lip balm and carefully applied it to her lips. The smell of watermelons filled the room, and I realized it was my mom's lip balm.

"So, like, how long are you staying here?" asked the girl.

My mom picked up a small nylon wallet and shoved it into her back pocket. "Just a few more days. My mom will be back on Thursday."

I remembered that my mom's mother, Diana—my own grandmother—would have been recently divorced at this point. I remembered my dad telling me that my mom and grandmother had moved to a house on the outskirts of Stellamar for just a year or so while my grandmother pulled herself together after her divorce, before they moved to Connecticut. I had asked my dad why they hadn't just moved in with Lady Azura, since her house was so big, and my dad had explained that my grandmother didn't have the best relationship with Lady Azura.

"I bet you can't wait to leave," the girl said in a snide voice. "This old house gives me the creeps. I don't know how you can stay here!"

I watched my mom carefully, waiting for her to say something to defend Lady Azura's house. Her cheeks got red, so I knew the comment bothered her on some level, but she didn't say anything. Instead she just changed the subject.

"So, Julie," she said in a fake cheerful voice, as if her grandmother's home hadn't just been insulted. "I was thinking about what to wear for the first day of school, and I—" She stopped suddenly.

Wailing. Weeping. The sounds were coming from the pink bedroom next door. I knew who it was. A spirit. The spirit of a young mother who'd lived a long time ago. She had lost her child to a bad illness. When I'd first moved into my great-grandmother's house, I'd heard the wailing spirit a lot. Nowadays she didn't cry quite so much, because she and I had figured out together how she could be reunited with her little boy, at least some of the time. But she was crying now.

My mother could hear the spirit.

The realization struck me all at once. I watched in a daze as my mom walked over to the dresser and snapped on the huge boom box. Loud music blared into the room.

She was trying to drown out the sound of the spirit.

It was clear to me, if not to my mother, that Julie could not hear the spirit, but she was looking at my mom a little strangely. I knew that look well. I had gotten it from my own friends plenty of times when I had done something random in a panic to cover up the presence of a spirit. Then Julie motioned to the window. "My mom is here. Finally! Let's go!"

Through a fog, I heard my father calling me. The vision ended. I was back in my room, staring down at the loopy purple handwriting in my mother's diary.

. . . so Julie and I went to the mall. I bought a cool new shirt and a headband with a bow to wear to the dance.

I can't wait till Mom comes back to get me. I don't like it here. Julie's right . . . it's creepy. I don't know what the deal is with all the weird sounds, but I'm just glad Julie didn't seem to hear them. I don't want her to tell everyone at school that my grandmother lives in a creepy old house. That would definitely not be cool.

The entry ended.

I heard my dad call again, and I called back that I'd be right down.

My thoughts were swirling. My mother had powers. I knew from the vision that she could definitely hear spirits. I had been able to see them long before I could hear them. Was it the same for my mom? Could she *see* them too?

Lady Azura had told me that my mother didn't have any powers. How was it possible that she never told anyone?

Then I realized I was jumping the gun. This was only beginning of the diary. I was sure that once I kept reading, I would find out what had really happened. My mom had wanted me to find this diary. I was sure that if I kept reading, I would find out what she wanted me to know.

She is sharing with me how she came to learn about and embrace her powers.

The thought rolled around inside my head and made me smile. My mom and I had even more in common than I had ever realized.

I'm just like her.

I decided I'd read enough for now. I would savor

the diary, reading it in small installments so I could draw it out for as long as possible. Kind of like the way I would eat a piece of tiramisu cake from my favorite bakery, Prudente's. One nibble at a time. I stashed the diary under my mattress, straightened the covers, and headed downstairs.

Chapter 3

My dad was standing in the front hallway, his jacket on, keys in his hand. He was dressed for going out. Pants that looked ironed. Blue shirt tucked in. He'd even shaved.

"You ready, kiddo?" he called when he saw me at the top of the stairs.

I almost asked him what he was talking about, and then I realized it was nearly six. I had a date tonight with Mason. Well, sort of a date. We were meeting at Lenny's and having pizza together and then hanging out. My dad was supposed to drive me.

I'd been looking forward to this date with Mason big-time, so it was a little hard to believe I had almost forgotten about it. But I guess the diary trumped Mason, even if he was the cutest boy at school. (In my opinion. Lily's crush, Cal, was also supercute, but to be honest I found him a little boring to talk to.) I had been crushing on Mason for a while now, and it was starting to seem like maybe he liked me, too. I had promised Lily I would fill her in on every detail later tonight.

"Be right there!" I said, pivoting and returning to my room. There wasn't much I could do about my hair in two minutes, so I decided to throw it up in a loose bun. Lily always told me I looked good with my hair up. I dug through a drawer until I found a tube of lip gloss and put a light coating on my lips. I smiled as I remembered my mom putting lip balm on in my vision. I looked my outfit over carefully in the mirror. In jeans and a striped long-sleeved tee, I certainly couldn't be accused of looking overdressed. I wished I had Lily's fashion sense—she would probably be able to add some little accessory to my outfit, like a belt or bracelet, to make it look perfect. The only accessory I had on was the same one I always wore—my crystal necklace. But it was almost six, so my ensemble would have to do. Luckily, Mason was a casual kind of guy anyway. He always wore jeans and a random T-shirt and scuffed-up board sneakers. And besides, he was used to seeing me dressed like this. It would be totally weird to show up for pizza all decked out in a dress or something. At least I hoped so!

I ran down the stairs and smiled at my dad.

"Ready for your big pizza date?" he asked in a teasing voice. He knew all about Mason. I had told him we were meeting up for pizza, though I hadn't called it a date. I was secretly kind of glad my dad thought it was a date. I hoped he was right. I really wanted it to be a date.

I sniffed the air purposefully as we got into the car and buckled our seat belts. "I might ask you the same thing," I said. "It's not every day you wear the cologne I gave you for Christmas. You must have some big plans of your own. . . ."

I generally approved of my father dating. He'd never really gotten over my mother's death, I knew, but I didn't want him to be lonely. With a couple of notable exceptions, I usually liked the women he went on dates with.

"Not big plans," my dad answered as he drove the few blocks to Lenny's. "I've been invited to a dinner party at the Flanagans', but they did mention something about there being a nice single lady there they would like me to meet."

"Ah, so a blind date? Won't that be awkward?" I couldn't imagine being fixed up on a blind date. It was nerve-racking enough to be on my way to meet Mason for pizza! I was glad that blind dates were only something older people did.

"No, not a date. Just a dinner party. I'm the convenient eligible male in a lot of people's address books in Stellamar, I've discovered." He grinned ruefully as we approached Lenny's. "I've accepted that it's easier to just go along with it than to try and protest."

"Okay, well . . . have fun tonight," I said as I unbuckled my seat belt and got out of the car. "I hope she turns out to be really nice."

"Thanks, kiddo. You have fun too. If Mason's mom can't drive you home and it's after dark, then call me and I'll come pick you up."

I told him I would.

Mason was waiting for me as I walked up to the door of Lenny's. I felt that familiar sensation when I was in his presence—dry mouth, sweaty palms, not sure where to look. He was really good-looking, but in an almost opposite-of-Jayden kind of way. Jayden had been my first crush. He'd moved away. He had been tall, dark, and handsome. Coffee eyes. Almond-colored skin. Chocolate-brown hair. Mason had almost white-blond hair and was fair-complexioned with green eyes. He blushed easily, like I did. He wasn't quite as tall as Jayden, but he had broad shoulders and an athletic walk.

I knew it was probably wrong to compare them. I'm sure I wouldn't like it if I knew Mason was comparing me to some other girl. But I did anyway. And it wasn't just a physical difference. Mason was different from Jayden in a lot of ways. With Jayden, I was always laughing and goofing around. Mason was more serious. I had always felt at ease with Jayden, and I can't say I ever really felt that way with Mason.

There was one really important detail about Mason. He and I had a special connection, one that I had not shared with Jayden.

Mason had powers too.

Not like mine. He couldn't see spirits, but he could move objects with his mind. Lady Azura called it telekinesis. He'd recently told his parents what he could do, but I was the only kid who knew about it. I had promised to keep it a secret for him, and I had. I hadn't even told Lily, though I sometimes wished I could, because it would help for her to know the whole story when I talked to her about Mason. But a promise was a promise, and I wasn't going to break mine.

Mason also knew about my powers. He had promised not to tell anyone about them either. I wasn't that worried about it. A year ago, it would have totally stressed me out to think a boy I liked knew my secret. I had been so worried Jayden was going to find out, though he never did. I managed to keep it hidden from him, even when the spirit of his brother, Marco, started showing up. That hadn't been easy to do.

But it didn't bother me now. Since I had told Lily what I could do, and she had totally accepted it, I felt way less anxiety over what everyone else would think of me if they knew.

"Hey," Mason said with a half smile. He looked quickly at me and then just as quickly looked away.

"Hey," I replied, also letting my gaze drop to the ground.

You see him all the time at school. You're just meeting for pizza. This is no big deal. Calm down and act like a normal person.

We stood in the doorway and looked inside at the bustling pizza place.

Finally I said, "It's cold out here."

"Yeah, sure is."

"Sooo . . . want to go in?"

"Oh. Yeah, sure."

We went in and sat down at a small booth away from the front door. It was warmer inside. I commented about it to Mason.

"Is it too warm? Are you hot?" he asked, looking around the restaurant as if to scope out a table in a cooler spot.

"No, this is fine. I just meant it's not cold in here like outside."

Mason nodded and then our conversation stalled until the waitress came over. We ordered a small plain pie to share and two sodas. Mason got root beer. I chose ginger ale. I racked my brains for something to talk about.

"So—"

"So—"

We both spoke at the same time, and then we both stopped. The large bottle of red pepper flakes fell over even though neither of us had touched it. Mason's face turned red, and he reached over to pick up the bottle.

"Sorry," he murmured.

"Don't worry about it," I said with a small smile.

"I sometimes can't help it," he explained. "The stuff my mind moves, that is."

"I get it," I said, trying to be reassuring. "I can't control when I see spirits, though I sometimes wish I *could* control it. And besides, I think it's pretty awesome that you can do it." And I meant it.

He shook his head, his expression darkening. "I don't. I really wish I could get rid of this—this problem. Just last week I saw Mr. Hoagland in the supermarket when I was there with my mom. I'd skipped his class that morning and gone to the nurse saying I didn't feel well, because I hadn't done the reading. I didn't want him to see me. To have him ask me about it in front of my mom."

I waited. He seemed to want to go on, but it also seemed to bother him to talk about the incident.

"Anyway, just like that, a huge pyramid of soup

cans went crashing to the floor and rolling all over the place. I made it happen. With my mind. But not on purpose. I just didn't want to see him, to have him ask me how I was feeling with my mom standing right there. But I hadn't meant to knock all those cans over. And some poor guy had to clean them up. I felt really bad about it."

He clamped his mouth shut as the waitress came over with our sodas.

I waited for him to continue, but he seemed to be finished with his story. I wasn't sure what to say.

"It wasn't your fault, Mason," I said finally.

He gave me a bewildered look. "Of course it was my fault. I did it. Don't you get that?"

"Well, I guess it was technically your fault, but you shouldn't beat yourself up about it. It was just some soup cans! Give it time. I'm sure you'll figure out how to control it." He seemed to be listening to what I was saying, so I kept going. "I'm getting better all the time dealing with the spirit stuff. My great-grandmother is helping me. You probably just need some practice."

"I don't want to practice," Mason replied, crumpling his straw wrapper in his fist, as if for emphasis. "I just want it to go away. All I do is worry that someone will find out," he said in a low voice. "I feel like a freak. We're quite the pair, you and I."

Was he calling me a freak? I was pretty sure he was. I didn't know how to respond to that, so I decided to change the subject.

"So have they said when you guys can get back to Harbor Isle?" I asked. Mason and a bunch of his classmates lived two towns over. Their school had been damaged in the hurricane we'd had a few weeks ago. That's why he was going to school in Stellamar.

He shook his head and shrugged. "Probably a few more months," he said. "They'll have us finish out the semester. Makes sense, I guess."

I nodded as the waitress came over with our pizza. It smelled delicious.

For a while we focused on our pizza. Lenny's has a lot of good stuff on every table you can add to your pizza— pepper flakes, oregano, even freshly grated parmesan cheese that comes in little bowls with spoons to sprinkle it on. I added liberal amounts of oregano and cheese. Mason ignored the extra toppings and dug right in.

We ate in near silence. A few times I tried starting

up a conversation, but Mason wasn't very talkative. I felt confused. I'd been so excited about this yesterday. But now that I was here, the energy between Mason and me seemed way off. Was it me? I felt a pang of longing for Jayden and tried to push him out of my mind. It really wasn't fair for me to be thinking about him while I was out with another boy . . . even if that boy was proving to be a not-very-fun dinner date.

After we ate, I suggested we walk down the block for ice cream at Scoops. It was only 6:40. It seemed like an embarrassingly short time to hang out together if we were really on what you'd call a date. Maybe we'd meet up with people we knew who could help move the conversation along. He looked a little hesitant. But then he agreed.

As we walked into Scoops, my heart sank. Across the restaurant, along the opposite wall, there was a booth with some girls we knew, but they weren't girls I particularly wanted to hang out with. They were all from Harbor Isle.

"Mason! Over here!" One of the girls sprang to her feet, waving wildly and gesturing toward her table. It was Jody Jenner.

Chapter 4

Jody was a classmate of Mason's from Harbor Isle, one of the kids who was attending Stellamar Middle School. She'd zoomed to the top of the popularity charts at Stellamar in no time flat, which I guess wasn't surprising, given her amazing looks and seemingly endless confidence. And the fact that kids thought her parents were ultracool. Her dad was a famous director. Her mom was a former model turned famous photographer. With the help of her parents and their many connections, Jody had organized a hurricane-relief fund-raiser auction, which had been wildly popular and raised a lot of money. She was the middle school equivalent of a queen.

I wanted to like Jody. In some ways, she reminded me of Lily—she was pretty, smart, and really outgoing. But unlike Lily, she wasn't always very nice. I couldn't shake the feeling that she didn't like me. And she and Lily definitely didn't like each other. I tried to stay neutral. Lily didn't mind conflict. I much preferred to avoid it.

And speaking of conflict, it was becoming pretty clear to me that Jody liked Mason. *Like*-liked him. Which, according to Lily, explained why she didn't like me. It was all very complicated.

"Hi, guys!" said Jody, her eyes trained on Mason. "Come join us!"

"Um . . . sure," Mason said. After he said it, he glanced over at me as if to ask if that was all right, but what was I going to say? I shrugged slightly, and he headed over to the booth. I recognized one of the other three girls sitting with Jody. Caroline something. I'd met her before. But I had never really spoken to the other two.

They all squished together to make room for Mason and me.

"So, can I get anyone ice cream?" Mason asked awkwardly. The three girls already had ice cream, so obviously he was talking just to me. But he was acting like it was just a general question to the group.

Was he trying to pretend we weren't here together?

The girls all exchanged looks with one another. One of them giggled.

"Um, we're good," said Jody, gesturing to the ice-cream dishes on the table. I squirmed uncomfortably in my seat, feeling my face get hot.

"Actually, I'm really full from dinner," I said. "I think I'll skip it this time."

Mason shrugged, like he didn't care whether I had ice cream, and headed off to the counter to order.

"So, Sara Collins," said Jody in a singsong tone. She leaned toward me across the table, her large eyes wide and probing. "Big date tonight?"

My face was most definitely red now. "What? Oh. Oh, not really," I stammered. "We're just, like, you know, hanging out. We had some pizza."

"Who asked who?" Jody asked sharply, her eyes narrowing.

"I don't remember. We just made plans," I said lamely, looking away. As soon as I said the words, I felt angry at myself for not telling her the truth—that Mason had asked me out and it was a date. At least it had been in my mind. But unlike Jody, I wasn't born with a ton of confidence. I kind of hate to admit it, but she intimidated me. I knew she liked him, and I knew she wouldn't want to hear that Mason liked me.

That is, if Mason even did like me. I wasn't too sure anymore.

Luckily, Mason returned just then. He was carrying a gigantic bowl of ice cream with three different scoops: vanilla, chocolate, and strawberry. He sat down and squirted a crown of whipped cream around the top of the dish, expertly moving in smaller and smaller circles until his ice cream was crowned with a huge mound of fluffy white cream. One of the girls at the end of the table shoved the rotating tray of toppings toward him, and we all watched in semi-horrified fascination as he spooned about seven different toppings onto his tower of whipped cream.

"So. Big news for you, Mace," Jody said, drumming her hands on the table.

"What news?" came Mason's muffled response as he downed a huge bite of topping-laden whipped cream.

"My dad is shooting the commercial on Tuesday."

"What commercial?" asked the girl with red hair

sitting next to me. I realized neither Mason nor Jody had introduced me to her, or to the girl to her right, who was busy texting.

"Didn't I tell you?" asked Jody. "My dad usually only directs movies or TV, but he's doing a twenty-second commercial spot that's going to air on the Rocker Channel. He has this amazing song he's going to use for the overdub, and guess who's going to be lip-synching it? *Moi*." She put a hand to her chest and lowered her eyes in mock modesty.

"Shut UP!" yelled Caroline, so loud that the people at the next booth turned around. "That is too awesome!"

"And guess who is going to play my 'love interest,' as my dad puts it? Mason said he would."

Mason rolled his eyes. "No, *you* said I would. I didn't agree to do it."

"Mace, puh-leeze say you'll do it?" pleaded Jody.

"I'd never hear the end of it from the guys," Mason replied, his cheeks turning a little pink at the thought of it.

"I think it would be totally awesome," said the girl with the red hair, practically swooning in her seat.

"Wouldn't it be so awesome, Candace?" she asked, nudging the girl to her right.

The girl paused in her texting and nodded without looking up. "Totally awesome."

There was a brief silence, and I felt as though everyone around the table was looking at me, waiting for me to say something. Everyone but Mason, who had renewed his attack on his sundae tower.

"Yeah, sounds like it would be a pretty cool thing to do," I said lamely.

"You don't even have to sing or talk or say a thing," Jody told Mason. "You just have to stand there and look cute. Shouldn't be too hard for you."

The other three girls giggled.

"Yeah, okay," grumbled Mason. "So tell me the details. When I have to be there and stuff."

Jody and Mason leaned toward each other across the table and started discussing details. My eyes wandered around Scoops. At one point the texting girl looked up and I tried to smile at her, and I'm pretty sure she rolled her eyes at me. I'd never wished so much to have Lily with me. She would know how to handle this situation. Thinking of Lily, I remembered

I hadn't called her. She'd said she had some big, important thing to talk to me about, and I had totally forgotten about her.

"Um, I have to make a call," I mumbled, sliding out of the booth and heading toward the back of the restaurant, where it was a little quieter. Mason and Jody had barely looked up.

"Lil," I said, when she answered. "Sorry. I meant to call before."

"That's okay," said Lily. She was always so cheerful and upbeat. "I know you've been pretty busy today. I'm home. Babysitting. How's your date with Mason?"

I glanced across the restaurant at Mason, who was still engrossed in a conversation with Jody.

"Fine, I guess," I said. "We ran into Jody and her friends at Scoops and got stuck sitting with them."

"Ugh."

"Yeah, I think the date is pretty much over at this point, and 'ugh' about sums things up. Do you want me to come over?"

"That'd be awesome, but I don't want to wreck your evening."

"Not to worry. It will be a good excuse to leave," I

said. "I was so excited about this date with him yesterday. But now, I don't know. The magic seems to have gone away. Maybe I'm just distracted because of the diary."

"So how is the diary?" Lily asked eagerly.

I hesitated. Part of me wanted to tell her everything, but part of me didn't want to talk about it. I wasn't sure I wanted to share what I had learned about my mom just yet. Not even with Lily.

"Why don't I come over soon and we'll talk about everything?" I said. "Unless something changes drastically when I get back to the table, I think it would be totally fine for me to bow out early. It's barely past seven. This might end up being the shortest date in history."

Lily said she'd speed up the process of getting her little sister, Cammie, to bed, so she'd be ready for me when I got there.

I moved back to the booth, where Mason and Jody and the others were still engaged in a lively conversation. As I sat there, I kept thinking of my mom, and how I had found out that she could see spirits. Everything else suddenly just seemed not that important. It reminded me of one of my favorite photos that my mom had taken. It was a red cardinal on the branch of a tree in early spring. The brilliant red of the bird made everything around it look washed out and gray. That's how I felt about my mom's diary. It was like that red cardinal. The stuff with Mason felt like the gray landscape.

"Um, hey," I said, interrupting their conversation. Mason looked at me, guiltily, I thought, like I'd caught him doing something wrong. "I'm going to go," I said simply. "I'll see you guys in school on Monday?"

The napkin dispenser at our table suddenly fell over.

Mason scrambled to his feet. "I'll walk you home," he said.

"No, no, it's totally fine," I said. "It's not even dark out yet. I'm good." I waved to everyone, hoping it didn't look like I was leaving in a huff, and headed to the door.

Mason followed me to the front entrance anyway.

As soon as we stepped outside, I felt the chill. It had grown colder. I pulled my jacket tightly around myself and hugged my arms around my waist.

"Are you, like, mad?" he asked me. His eyes looked

every which way, except at me.

Out of the corner of my eye, I saw a spirit hovering behind Mason. I'd pretty much grown used to seeing spirits at random times, so it didn't startle me. Much. But it did catch my attention, and it probably looked to Mason like I was purposely ignoring him.

"Um, Sara? Listen, I'm sorry," he said, the words tumbling out of his mouth quickly. "I didn't mean for our night to get all hijacked like that. . . ."

He looked upset. He meant it. I decided I really wasn't mad. Maybe I should be, but I wasn't. "It's fine. I just need to get home. But I'm not mad."

He looked relieved.

"You go on back inside. I'll see you soon."

I stepped away before there could be any awkwardness about him kissing me good-bye.

I waited for him to go inside, and then I walked around to see if I could find the spirit I'd seen. I'd had the impression he had been waiting there for me. He was gone, but I remembered what he had looked like.

A young man, or maybe he had been a teenager. It had been hard to tell. Dressed in old-fashioned clothes. Glowing dimly in the growing darkness. A stained, dirty work shirt. Pants tied at the waist with a rope. Heavy work boots. Long hair that flopped over one eye. A beret on his head.

I had no idea who he was or why he was there, but as I walked home, I couldn't shake the feeling that he had wanted to tell me something.

Chapter 5

I knocked quietly on Lily's kitchen door so as not to wake her little sister, but Buddy, the Randazzos' dog, started barking his head off like crazy.

Lily opened the door quickly and shushed Buddy, who recognized me right away. He wagged his tail wildly and rammed his head into my legs so I would pet him, which I did.

"Cammie's asleep and the boys are upstairs watching a movie," said Lily, dropping wearily into a chair. "Help yourself to anything you want."

Lily and I knew our way around each other's kitchens like they were our own. "I'm good," I said. I pulled up another chair and sat down next to her at the large, battered kitchen table. I loved Lily's kitchen. Large, light, and airy, and almost always bustling with people. Mrs. Randazzo was an amazing cook, so it was usually full of the smells of home cooking.

"So what's going on?" I asked, getting right down to it. "What's the big important thing you wanted to tell me about?"

Lily's usually smiling face clouded up. She plucked a paper napkin from the holder and began twisting off little pieces, rolling them distractedly between her fingers. "My parents had a big fight."

"Oh," I said quietly. "That's awful. Are you okay?" I couldn't imagine Mr. and Mrs. Randazzo fighting. They always seemed to get along perfectly. I liked to think that's how my mom and dad would be, if my mom was still alive.

Lily shook her head. "Not like a *really* bad kind of fight. More like an argument. But it was about money. It wasn't good. See, my dad wants to enter into kind of a sketchy business deal."

That brought to mind gangsters and briefcases filled with cash. I'd been watching too many detective shows on TV recently. "Like, something illegal?"

"No," Lily scoffed, and waved her hand as if the idea of her dad doing something illegal was silly. Which, of course, it was. "Sketchy according to my mom. You know that vacant lot at the end of Culver Street, way at the other end of the boardwalk?"

"You mean that dirt field near the old railroad tracks?"

"Yep. That one. Well, I guess this developer friend of my dad is in some financial trouble, so he offered to sell it to my dad for way cheap. And my dad wants to buy it and develop it into a little shopping area, with touristy stores and stuff. But my mom says it's crazy. See, as long as our family has lived here, and you know that's a very long time, no one has ever had success building on that spot."

"That's odd," I said. "Because you'd think it would be a great place for shops and stuff. It's right at the end of the boardwalk, and there's that really nice old inn just half a block toward the water."

"I know, right? But see, I think the spot is jinxed. My mom definitely thinks so too, even though she didn't use that actual word. Apparently people did try to build on it in the past, my mom says. But things just kept going wrong."

"What kinds of things?"

"Different stuff. One guy went bankrupt before he even started construction. Someone else built a restaurant, but it burned down before it even opened its doors. Someone else tried to just make it a parking lot, but weird stuff kept happening to the construction equipment, and the workers all quit."

"Why does your dad want it then?"

"He just refuses to believe the superstitious stuff. You know how he is. But I heard them talking about how he's dipped into our savings and we could lose a lot—a ton—of money if it doesn't work out. He's supposed to sign the contract in a few weeks and leave some massive deposit. I'm getting really nervous about it, Sar. What should I do?"

I felt bad for Lily. But I had no clue what to say. Land deals and lawyers and developments and business transactions all sounded pretty grown-up to me. I didn't want to give her bad advice.

"I'm sure it will all work out," I said, trying to sound encouraging. "I mean, your dad is really smart. I'm sure he wouldn't do anything that wasn't a good idea."

Judging from the look on Lily's face, I had said the wrong thing.

"But what about the jinx?" she demanded.

I didn't want to point out to her that we had no way of knowing if there really was a jinx or not. I needed to be supportive. "Can you tell me more about what you know about it?" I asked, thinking that if I kept her talking about it, I'd come up with something helpful to say.

So Lily told me everything she knew again. She was really animated, and it was clear that the more she talked about it, the more she became convinced that this deal was going to result in disaster.

I definitely wasn't helping. When she was done, I still didn't know what to say, so I repeated the same unhelpful thing I had said before, that I was sure everything would work out okay.

"I guess I should get going," I said a little while later.

"I guess I should get the boys to bed anyway," Lily said quietly. I had let her down and I knew it. I just didn't know how to help.

I left soon after that. I think we both felt bad about the way the evening had gone. I realized as I closed the door behind me that we hadn't even talked about our crushes. I had no clue what was going on between Lily and Cal.

It was definitely dark out now, but it was still before my curfew. The moon was out, so I could see my way, even between streetlamps. The wind had picked up, and dry leaves eddied and whirled across the sidewalk. I kept my eye out for the spirit of that young man I'd seen earlier, but sensed no one.

As I walked to my house—just two doors down from Lily's—I felt something near my collarbone. My hand went to my neck.

It was my necklace.

It was vibrating. Or, to be more specific, one of the crystals on it was vibrating.

I pulled it out of the top of my shirt and stared down at it. It was just long enough for me to see the small crystals strung on it. They were crystals Lady Azura had given me. People complimented me on my necklace all the time. They really did look pretty strung together. I knew them by heart, and by their feel: ruby, aquamarine, hematite, opal, tourmaline, moldavite, diamond, quartz, and aragonite. Each one had a meaning, which Lady Azura had explained to me. And one of them was vibrating. It felt hot to the touch.

It was the ruby.

The ruby crystal was the first one Lady Azura had ever given me. At the time, she told me it would encourage love to bloom. She gave it to me and I had my first vision of Jayden. For weeks after that, I depended on the crystal to help me. And it turned out Jayden had liked me, too. I didn't think it was entirely because of the ruby crystal that Jayden had liked me back, but I believed it had helped.

Was it trying to tell me something now, about Mason? Did it know that I was confused about Mason and it was trying to help again? Maybe my body gave off those vibes, and the ruby "sensed" them somehow. I would have to ask Lady Azura. In general terms, of course. As great as Lady Azura was, I wasn't eager to start discussing the details of my love life with her.

She was standing in the kitchen when I walked in a few minutes later, almost as if she'd been waiting for me.

My great-grandmother was a tiny person. Maybe four inches shorter than I was. Reed thin. But for such a small person, she had a huge presence. I'd been in crowded rooms with her, and she somehow managed to command the attention of the room. Some people just do that. They give off energy. Your eye is just drawn to them.

Although it was nearly ten, she was still fully dressed. Flowing silk skirt, a dark pink blouse, and a scarf tied around her head, covering her dyed mahogany-colored hair. Ropes of necklaces. Dramatic red lipstick. And I could smell her perfume from across the kitchen.

"Sara, I'm so glad you're home," she said.

"Is everything okay?" I asked anxiously. She seemed distressed. "Is my dad okay?"

"He's fine. Your father hasn't returned from his dinner party yet," she reassured me. "I am glad you're home because I need your help with something."

I set down my bag and pulled off my jacket. "What's going on?"

"It's the spirit upstairs in the pink bedroom. She's been terribly upset tonight."

"Wait, so you actually *heard* her?" I asked Lady Azura, unable to hide my disbelief. Lady Azura was, as my dad put it, "hard of hearing." She could hear you when you talked to her, and she could hear the television or the phone, but her hearing wasn't as keen as that of a young person. And I knew for a fact that she couldn't always hear the spirits who were right in front of her, let alone the ones on the second floor.

Lady Azura gave me a look before she responded that told me she didn't like to be reminded of her hearing problems. "No, Sara, I cannot actually hear her. But I can sense her. I can sense there is a troubled energy coming from that part of the house, and I believe it to be coming from her."

So that explained it.

"Will you speak with her?" asked my great-grandmother. "As you know, I have such trouble climbing all those steep stairs. And you and she seem to have a connection. I would like for you to check in on her."

"Of course I will," I promised. "Why do you think she's started in again all of a sudden?"

Lady Azura shrugged her narrow shoulders. "I sense a disturbance in the atmosphere of some sort," she said. "But as yet I can't identify it. Possibly that's contributing."

Chapter 6

When I got to the top of the stairs, I didn't hear any loud sobbing, but there was definitely the sound of faint moaning and crying coming from the pink bedroom. I knocked quietly on the door, which was partially ajar, and slipped inside.

I felt a tickling at my collarbone. My ruby crystal. It was vibrating again. Maybe it was a sign that I should use it now, somehow. Although I had no idea how a crystal intended to make love bloom could help me now, with this heartbroken spirit.

The room was dark except for a thin, silvery light coming in through the window. The wind outside was seeping through the window jamb, and the draperies danced and rippled a little. I could see the silhouette of the spirit, rocking back and forth in her chair, her back to the door. Her features were in shadow, but I could see a light glowing around her. I moved across the room and sat down quietly on the seat cushion in the window and waited, not sure what to say or how to start.

"The very worst thing that can happen," she said softly, "is for a mother to lose a child." Her voice was thin and tremulous. She didn't really seem to be speaking to me directly. I had the feeling it almost didn't matter if I was there or not. But I responded anyway.

"I don't have a child, so I don't know," I said. "But I think you must be right." I considered saying that maybe the second worst thing is for a child to lose her mother too soon. Like I had. But I didn't say that. Because somehow it didn't seem right to say it. I couldn't think what to say instead, though. So I just sat there and waited for her to speak. To tell me why she was so upset about this again, after she seemed to have found peace.

But she didn't say anything else. She just buried her pale face in her ghostly hands and sobbed quietly, her black hair tumbling forward, her shoulders shaking.

I shifted uncomfortably. I had to come up with something. In books I had read about how people would say "there, there" to console someone. I'd never in my life said it before, but I tried it now.

"There, there," I said, immediately feeling dumb. But it seemed to help a little. At least, her sobs grew quieter. "You will see him again. Your boy. I've seen you together. You told me his name. Angus."

I realized what was probably happening. Lady Azura had told me that spirits sometimes exist in cycles. They can be in one cycle for a long time, and then suddenly the next day they are in a new cycle, and they have no memory of what happened in the last cycle. It was like having mini lifetimes over and over again. It had happened with the sailor spirit in the blue bedroom, though his cycles seemed to be very short. One week he was an old man who remembered my mom, and the next week he was a young man with no memory of her at all, because he had only known her as the spirit of an older man.

"Angus." She whispered the name in a low, hoarse voice. Her crying stopped abruptly. Her head jerked up. She stared at me with her deep eyes. They were like dark pools with no bottom.

"How say you?" she asked.

I realized she didn't even know who I was anymore. "How, uh, say I? I say me because—" I stopped. Tried again. "I am saying so because I've seen you with him. You see, these things just kind of come in cycles. You can usually see him, in the other cycle, but now you're in this cycle where you can't see him for some reason. But I'm not sure why." I wasn't explaining this right. I took a breath and tried again. "For a long time you couldn't see him and that made you sad, like you are now. But then you figured out what you needed to do, and you were reunited with him. He's usually with you, and that makes you happy. But there's some weird pressure thing happening in the atmosphere, and I think that's what's keeping you and Angus apart right now. I'm pretty sure." And I *was* pretty sure about it. I had no way of knowing it for certain, yet I felt strongly I was right.

"You have given me hope," she said, her voice now level, without any tremble. "Thank you."

She seemed to recover. Stopped crying. Just sat there rocking back and forth, back and forth.

I stole quietly out of the room. I went downstairs to report to Lady Azura, but she'd gone to bed. I saw my father's jacket on the hook, and, in the dim light outside, that his truck was parked near the shed. He must have returned while I'd been upstairs. The lights were out and the doors locked, so I headed upstairs.

I tapped on his door, then opened it. His light was on.

"Hey, kiddo," he said, emerging from his bathroom in his pj's, with a towel around his neck. He looked tired. "Have fun tonight?"

"Yeah, it was so-so," I said. "You?"

He grinned. "Just like I predicted, the Flanagans parked me next to a recently divorced woman. Very nice. But all she talked about was her ex-husband, so it wasn't a love connection. But they served really delicious seafood stew, so the night wasn't a total wash."

I smiled. Gave him a hug. Said good night.

It was very late when I finally climbed into my bed. Eager as I was to keep reading the diary, I didn't feel like my mind was alert enough to pay attention to every detail, and I didn't want to miss anything. I decided to wait until the next morning to continue reading.

I turned out my light, and the silvery moonlight bathed the room. I fell asleep to the sound of the wind howling outside.

Chapter 7

I woke up before nine the next morning, Sunday. Immediately I pulled the diary out from its hiding place. The floor was chilly under my bare feet. I climbed back under the covers to read it.

The first few entries were each about a page long. Then they shortened up to just a couple of sentences each day. That made sense. When you begin a diary or journal, you often have high hopes for yourself and your ability to keep the writing going. But still. It was impressive how long she'd kept it up. She had to have maintained it for at least a year, I thought. The writing was loopy and girlish, with the occasional i dotted with a heart.

August 19, 1984

School starts in two weeks, and I can't wait. I

have grown half an inch since the last time I measured myself about three weeks ago!!! Mom just announced she has to go away again. She leaves in two days. I'm happy that she loves her work so much, but it stinks how much she has to go away. This time, though, my grandmother is coming to my house to stay, rather than me going to her. That's good. I won't have to worry about dealing with you-know-what.

August 20
Last night Julie told me that she thinks Eric likes me. More later. Mom calling. I think my grandmother has just arrived.

August 21
Mom left this morning. I think it will be fun having Lady Azura stay with me. She brought a big stash of cookies and candy, which is awesome because my mom doesn't usually let us have a lot of sweets in the house. I told Lady Azura that, and she said that a little bit of sugar never hurt anyone. I don't know how she and my mom are related. They are so different!

I wonder sometimes if my mom ever saw or heard

anything growing up in that house. Ghosts. Spirits. Whatever you want to call them. I know I can't ask my mom about it because she'd freak. Am I crazy, Diary? Should I talk to Julie about this, or will she think I'm a psycho?

"No!" I wanted to shout at the page. I knew that talking to Julie was a terrible idea. From what I had seen of her in my vision, she didn't seem like the open-minded sort. My mom was insecure enough about her powers—telling a friend like Julie and having her judge her for them would make everything so much worse.

I closed the diary in my lap and thought about why my mom hadn't just confided in Lady Azura. She had the perfect person to talk to right there with her. Why not do something about it?

I knew my mom would do the right thing. So I kept reading.

August 22
Julie has the cutest clothes, but I have the worst clothes. Everything I have is so boring. Maybe

I should borrow some crazy stuff from Lady Azura's closet, ha-ha.

I smiled at the mention of Lady Azura's clothes. Age had definitely not mellowed her fashion sense.

My mom thinks Lady Azura's clothes are weird. I used to think they were kind of cool, but Julie told me she'd be mortified if her grandmother dressed like that, so I guess they're not very cool after all.

I stopped smiling.

August 23
Turns out Eric does not like me. He likes Stephanie. I am sure of this. At the roller rink he asked her to be skate partners even though I was standing two feet away. I also heard Carly ask him what kind of hair he likes on a girl and he said "curly." Stephanie has curly hair. So does Julie. My hair is stick straight. Maybe Mom will let me get a perm?

I read a few more pages and then closed the diary again. Tried to swallow the feeling of disappointment rising in me. My mom wasn't the way I had imagined her to be. I didn't like that she was so easily influenced by her stupid friend, Julie. I had imagined her to be really confident, like Lily.

Like how I knew I was deep down. I just had a hard time showing it sometimes.

My phone buzzed. It was a text from Lily.

GANG IS MEETING AT ARCADE AT 11. PLZ COME! M AND C WILL BE THERE. AM OUT DOING ERRANDS WITH MOM BUT CAN MEET YOU THERE!

The thought of seeing Mason made my heart flutter just a little bit. Did that mean maybe I did still like him? Or was I just anxious about seeing him again after our weird good-bye outside Scoops?

I texted her back.

OK! SEE YOU THERE!

I climbed out of bed and put the diary back in its hiding place under the mattress. I would read more later. Hopefully things would pick up.

I ate breakfast and helped my dad unload a pile of wood from the back of his truck. Then he gave me twenty dollars for the arcade. I protested, telling him I only needed ten at most, but he told me to just keep the change and save it for the next time I went out with my friends.

Since I had some time to get myself ready this time, I put a little more thought into my outfit. I decided I'd wear my black skinny jeans and a pink-and-white polka-dotted sweater that I had bought at the mall with Lily a few weeks ago. After taking a shower and dressing, I stood in front of the mirror, trying to decide what to do with my hair. I didn't know much about hairstyling before I met Lily, but Lily had introduced me to the fact that my hair had a pretty nice natural wave to it if I used the right styling stuff. That's usually how I wore my hair when I wanted to look nice—wavy. I started to spritz the beach-wave spray on my hair but stopped. I thought about my mom and her complaints about her stick-straight hair, and I decided I'd wear my hair nice and straight today. Just like my mom.

It was close to eleven when I left for the arcade, but it was a short walk. The place was right on the board-walk, just a few doors down from Scoops.

As I turned onto Beach Drive, the wind gusted off the water, whipping my hair around my face. So much for carefully styling it. But the late-September weather was warmer today, and the ocean sparkled in the fall sunlight. I stopped to look at the slate-gray water and the dramatic clouds hovering low over the horizon. I wished I'd brought my camera with me.

"'Scuse me, miss," said a gruff voice over my shoulder.

I whirled around.

It was the spirit of a young man. But not the same one I'd seen the night before. He was about the same age, though, and similarly dressed in knee-length pants cinched at the waist with a rope belt. This young man's skin was dark brown, his eyes coal black. He kneaded a cap between his hands and looked at me with anxious eyes.

"Please, miss, you mustn't allow it," he said. His voice was low and velvety-sounding, but I could hear the urgency in his tone.

"Allow what?" I asked him.

"It's dangerous," he continued, ignoring my question. "I know, miss, because I was there when it happened."

"Please," I said. "When *what* happened?"

"So many died," he went on, his eyes staring past me at some unseen, troubling memory.

"It sounds like you're trying to warn me about something, but see, I'm not sure what it is that—" I stopped speaking abruptly. Closed my mouth. Felt my face get hot and no doubt turn bright pink.

The spirit vanished.

Just behind him stood Jody Jenner.

She blinked at me curiously. Raised her eyebrows as if to ask me to explain myself and my weird behavior.

I couldn't think of anything to say. My mind went blank. She'd just observed me talking to thin air. And this was not the first time it had happened. Just last week, she'd caught me in the middle of a conversation with Mr. Barkus, the spirit of a long-dead gym teacher at my school. Lily had been there and had covered for me. We'd pretended I was reciting a poem I was memorizing for English.

"Oh, hi," I said.

"Hiiiii," she said, drawing the word out.

Silence. I couldn't use the poetry reason again.

So I just decided to pretend it hadn't happened. I really didn't have to explain myself to Jody Jenner.

"Are you heading to the arcade too?" I asked brightly. We were just half a block from it.

She nodded.

"Great. Let's go then."

"Oh," she said. And then a moment later she added, "Kaaay." We walked there in silence. It was awkward.

"Saraaaaaa!" yelled Lily from across the arcade as Jody and I walked in together. It was off-season in Stellamar, so the arcade wasn't all that crowded. My friends almost had the place to themselves. I spotted six or seven people I knew, scattered around at various games.

Mason was there. Standing next to Cal over at the basketball-shooting game. Watching Cal shoot as many baskets as he could before the clock ticked down. Had he seen me?

Lily was making her way across the room to meet me. Jody's friend Caroline bounded over to Jody and dragged her over to the dance machine.

"So how is it?" asked Lily.

"How is what?" I asked, baffled.

She looked both ways, then leaned in and said, "The diary! I am so sorry I forgot to ask you about it last night! Are you learning all kinds of amazing stuff about her?"

"Oh. That. Yeah, it's good," I said, but I knew I wasn't all that enthusiastic-sounding.

Lily raised her eyebrows. I wanted to explain, but it just wasn't the time or the place. I looked at my shoes.

"So will you come with me to see the site?" Lily asked, changing the subject.

Once again, I gave her a blank look. I had no clue what she was talking about.

Now her eyebrows knit together in a frown. "The place my dad wants to buy?" she prompted. "The one I told you about? The jinxed place?"

Of course. I should have figured that was what she meant. "I'm so sorry, Lil," I said, and I genuinely was. "It's been such a crazy day, and I just saw a spirit outside, and then Jody saw me talking to him, so I'm just all thrown off. Sure. I'll come with you to see it."

She smiled, but I wondered if I had hurt her feelings by not knowing immediately what she'd been talking about.

"Did you see Mason over there? And Cal? They're both here together. Are we going over there to talk to them? Or waiting for them to come talk to us?"

I glanced past Lily toward where Mason and Cal were standing.

"Neither," I said. "They're both talking to Jody and Caroline."

Lily's expression darkened. "What is up with that?" she demanded. "I heard that Jody was already going out with someone. A ninth grader. And Caroline is going out with what's-his-name from Harbor Isle. The kid with that hair." Lily made a sweeping motion across her forehead and I knew exactly what she meant, though I also couldn't remember the boy's name. "Why are they always hanging around our crushes?"

I shrugged. "Our crushes aren't exactly rushing over here to hang out with us," I pointed out. "Maybe they really are just friends. They all go to the same school. It must be kind of hard to get dumped into a new school for a semester, and they're just hanging together. Whatever. To be honest, I'm not even sure how I feel about Mason anymore."

Lily's eyebrows shot up. "Really? Do tell! Was it that bad last night?"

I wasn't sure what to say. I couldn't sort out my

feelings for Mason—all I knew was that I was confused. So I told Lily the truth. "I know this is kind of crazy, but I keep thinking about Jayden. He's been on my mind a lot."

She cocked her head to one side, giving me a sympathetic look. "Come on," she said suddenly, as if she had made up her mind about something. "Let's go play skee-ball with Marlee and Avery. And if our crushes don't come find us, then it's totally their loss! We are so not approaching them! Let's go have fun."

She turned and headed toward our friends.

As I started to follow her, I suddenly realized Mason was standing next to me. Where had he come from?

"Hi," I said, feeling super awkward.

"Hey," he replied. "I was hoping you'd show up."

"Yeah," I said. That was nice to hear. "How's it going over at the basketball?"

"Lousy," he said. "You'd think with my, ah, skill, I'd be able to score every time. But I can't control it that easily. However, I can make sure other people's balls don't go in, and even though I try not to, I still make that happen. It isn't fair, and there's nothing I can do to control it."

"Maybe if you practiced . . ."

"I don't want to," he said quickly, with some heat. "Anyway, I don't want to talk about it."

"Um, you brought it up." I hadn't meant for it to come out sounding quite so snotty, but it did anyway. Mason grimaced, and I felt bad.

"Mason! You're up!" yelled Cal from the basketball area.

"Go ahead," I said giving him a playful little shove. "I'm supposed to go play skee-ball anyway."

He smiled at me, unsure, but headed over to his friends.

I stayed at the arcade for about half an hour, but my heart wasn't really in it. My mind kept wandering to my mom. I felt like talking with Lady Azura. I wasn't ready to tell her about the diary yet, but I wanted to know what else she knew about my mom. Duggan had told me that my mom had wanted me to find the diary. So far I couldn't figure out what my mom wanted to tell me. Maybe Lady Azura could put me on track. Once I decided to talk to her about it, I felt like I couldn't get home fast enough.

I told my friends I was leaving. Lily's eyes clouded

over with disappointment, and I realized I'd promised her I'd go with her to see the site of her dad's business deal.

"I haven't forgotten, Lil," I said to her in a low voice, so others wouldn't hear. "It's just that I need to get home now to talk to Lady Azura. Can we go later this afternoon? He's not signing the paperwork for a few weeks, right?"

She nodded, and I told her I'd text her later.

I was halfway to the corner when I saw another spirit.

Chapter 8

Another young man. Same sort of clothing. But instead of a rope belt, his canvas trousers were held up by suspenders. He wore a work shirt the same color—drab green—as his pants. And a cap on his head. But I could see that he had red hair. He was leaning on a shovel. That made me think he was some sort of construction worker. But a hat instead of a helmet? Maybe that was what they wore a long time ago.

"Begging yer pardon, miss," he said to me. He had a very strong, lilting accent.

I stopped. Swallowed hard. I'd learned—thanks to Lady Azura—not to run away from spirits. To listen to what they wanted to tell me. Even though sometimes they didn't seem to know themselves what it was that was bothering them.

This one turned out to be that sort of spirit. I

couldn't get him to tell me specifically what it was he wanted.

"Yes?" I said, trying to look encouraging. "Do you want to tell me something?"

"The noise. The dust. Water came a-rushing in. Raight fearful. We lads knew 'twas our time. Then all went black," he said, his chin starting to quiver. He didn't look much older than sixteen or seventeen. I felt a pang of sadness. He had died so young.

"What happened?" I asked him.

"'Twasn't safe. 'Twasn't sound. He must hearken."

"Hearken?"

"Pay heed."

"*Who* must hearken? Please, I need to know more information. Can you just tell me—"

But the spirit shimmered and vanished before my very eyes. I stood there for a few minutes, hoping he would come back. I desperately wanted him to. I can't explain why, but I was suddenly pretty sure that these spirits I'd been seeing near the boardwalk had something to do with Lily's dad and his business deal. The idea just popped into my head, and the more I thought about it, the more I felt I was right. Finally I gave up and headed home, speed-walking the whole way.

Five minutes later I barreled into the house, determined to find Lady Azura.

I found her sitting at the kitchen table, spooning sugar into her dainty china cup of steaming tea.

"Come and sit," she commanded, waving her small, manicured hand laden with several heavy rings in the direction of the chair across from her.

I sat.

"Something is bothering you," she said. It was a statement. Not a question. She stared at me with her large, honey-brown eyes. "Tell me."

All thoughts of talking to her about my mother flew out of my head. Lily's problem felt much more urgent.

"Lily's dad is about to enter into a risky business deal," I said. "He wants to buy that vacant lot over on Culver Street, just off the boardwalk. Do you know it?"

She nodded, stirring her tea thoughtfully. "The site of the old Stellamar Junction, I believe my mother told me. That was where the depot used to be a hundred years ago. It's been vacant a long time. I have a dim recollection of a construction project starting there some years ago, but then it stopped. Nothing was built."

I nodded. "That's what Lily said too."

"Hmm. And as I think of it, I believe there was a restaurant there that burned down about twenty years ago."

"I think there were quite a few attempts to start businesses there," I said. "That's just it. According to Lily, stuff just keeps going wrong. She is convinced the place is jinxed."

"I had heard that as well," said Lady Azura. I must have looked startled, because she reached over and patted my hand. "I don't believe in jinxes, Sara. There is always a root to a problem. One just has to find it."

I wasn't sure what she meant by that. Lady Azura often spoke in riddles. "Well, whatever it is, Lily's mom and dad have been arguing about it, because Lily's dad has decided to invest a lot of their savings into the deal and Mrs. Randazzo is all freaked out that they're going to lose everything. Lily keeps asking my opinion and advice, but that's grown-up stuff and I don't know what to say to her. I feel like I'm letting her down."

Lady Azura sipped her tea slowly. "I think your instinct is right not to get involved. I have had a great deal of experience with people seeking advice about financial matters. Expressing one's opinion on a financial matter, even if it's solicited, rarely ends well. People are very peculiar when it comes to money matters, Sara. You may tell them your opinion, but they usually do what they want to do anyway. The best thing you can do is to support Lily, to be there for her, to listen when she needs to talk. But that is all you can do."

I nodded. Watched her take another dainty sip of her tea. Her eyes gazed at me over the rim. "I sense there is more to this story. Tell me."

I took a deep breath and plunged in. "I've also been seeing spirits. Around the boardwalk. Young men, from a long time ago. I think they are trying to warn me about something, and I have this feeling it has to do with Lily's dad's deal, but I'm not sure why I think that. "

She set her teacup down carefully into the saucer. Folded her hands. Now she looked really interested. "Tell me more," she prompted.

I told her about the encounters I'd had with the young men. How they seemed to be trying to warn me, or to warn someone, about something. But that they kept vanishing before I could get them to tell me what they were worrying about. I told her that after talking to the last one, the one with the bright-red hair, I'd gotten the feeling that it was all somehow connected to Lily's father and the business deal.

"Quite interesting," she murmured. "You say they seem to belong together, perhaps from the same family or school?"

I shrugged. "Their clothes look alike. Not fancy clothes, but they're all about the same age, and from the same era. Too old for school, though. And not from the same family. They all speak with different accents and things. And none of them look alike."

"It sounds as if we need to conjure them," Lady Azura said firmly. "Perhaps we can find out what it is they are trying to tell you if you can talk to them in a more controlled setting. The atmospheric disturbances that are going on right now might explain why they cannot seem to stay around long enough to finish telling you whatever it is they have to say. It could also explain why your perception—your intuition—is heightened, if that is actually the case. But if it will be a few weeks before Lily's father signs his paperwork, there is plenty of time to find out more."

"That would be awesome," I said, feeling relieved. I loved that she always had answers for me, sometimes even before I knew what my questions were. And I loved that she trusted my intuition so much. I felt so lucky to have my great-grandmother as part of my life. "Can we do it right now?" I asked hopefully.

"Perhaps tomorrow after school," she said. "I am waiting for your father to take me to my hair appointment. And the rest of my day is booked. But we will deal with this soon."

Chapter 9

I spent the rest of the afternoon tackling my homework. My social studies assignment took me a lot longer than I thought it would, and when I looked at the clock it was almost dinnertime. I hurried downstairs. Sunday nights were my night to cook dinner. My dad always offered to help, but I actually really liked cooking. It made me feel good to spend time preparing food for my family to eat.

I tried a vegetable bean soup recipe Lily's mother had written out for me.

It was simple enough to make, but I spent a lot of time chopping vegetables. My shoulders ached from hunching over the big pot by the time the soup was finished. My dad and Lady Azura pronounced it delicious. It wasn't as good as Mrs. Randazzo's, but I was pretty happy with how it turned out. We ate it with pieces of crusty bread my dad had gotten from the bakery, and all in all it was a pretty good meal. My dad offered to do the dishes, which I gladly took him up on. I raced upstairs to my room and closed the door. Then I pulled out the diary and began reading where I'd left off.

Monday, September 3

Labor Day today. School starts tomorrow!!!! Mom has been away for five days, and I miss her so much. I wish I had someone to talk to. Last night Lady Azura and I had shortbread cookies and tea for dinner. Mom definitely would not approve, but like Lady Azura said, what she doesn't know won't hurt her.

I thought of the much healthier dinner I'd just had with my family and wondered if Lady Azura had been secretly wishing I'd serve cookies and tea one Sunday night.

Should I wear the blue button-down or the pink-striped shirt tomorrow? I was thinking the blue, but Julie said that pink plays up my tan better. I'll call her and see what she thinks.

I sighed and turned the page.

And then everything went a little fuzzy. I knew what was happening just before it happened. I was having another vision.

I was standing in the hallway of a school. My school. Stellamar Middle School. Same walls, same windows. But the lockers were different. These were pale green and beat-up, with built-in combination locks. And the kids rushing past me did not look like the students in my school. They were dressed in crazy outfits. Girls with high-waisted jeans and shirts with humongous shoulders, almost like football uniforms. Boys with long hair, pleated pants. No one seemed to have backpacks. The girls carried their books clasped against their chests. The boys carried theirs balanced on one hip.

There was no sign of my mother. But I knew from the way everyone was dressed that the era was the eighties. My mom's era for middle school.

The crowd thinned out—it must have been the rush between classes. And then I saw her. Alice. A spirit I had met last year, right after I had started at Stellamar Middle School. She had died decades before—even before this time I was in now. I had gotten to know Alice pretty well. She'd died very tragically, of a terrible illness. Polio. I had helped to clear her name, because the town had wrongly blamed her for bringing the illness to Stellamar.

I almost forgot I wasn't really there, that this was just a vision. I almost called out to Alice. But then I saw my mother.

It was clear that she had also seen Alice. Her face was white. She was breathing fast, like she'd just finished a sprint.

This confirmed it. My mother could see and hear spirits.

She was just like me.

The last thought I had before the vision abruptly ended was that she'd decided to wear the pink-striped shirt for her first day.

I took a few deep breaths and looked around my room. I realized that my heart was pounding.

Eager to read on, I stared down at the page again. And immediately plunged into a second vision.

I was standing on a playground with an asphalt surface. It was a warm afternoon, but the leaves on the tree overhanging the playground fence were orange and yellow, so I saw that it was fall. Then I recognized my school. The playground where I was now standing had been demolished since my mother's day to make way for the playing fields that were now in this area.

I spotted my mom. Same pink-striped shirt. It must be later that same day, I decided.

She and Julie were sitting side by side on the swing set, their heads bowed toward each other, having a conversation about something. I hurried over.

"Natalie," said Julie, "what are you talking about? You are making no sense."

"I don't know how else to say it, Julie," my mom said. She looked really upset, like she might start crying at any moment. My heart sank as I realized what they were talking about.

My mom had told Julie about seeing spirits.

"This can't end well," I said out loud, but of course they couldn't hear me. I stood and listened and watched, feeling like I was watching an accident unfold before my eyes and I was powerless to stop it.

The look on Julie's face said it all. She was looking

at my mom like she was crazy. But my mom either couldn't stop talking or didn't want to.

"They're people who aren't really there. You know, like *dead* people."

"DEAD people?" Julie repeated loudly, her eyebrows shooting up. My mother winced.

"Yeah, you know. Ghosts. I try to ignore them. But it seems to be happening more and more, and I just don't know what I should do. I saw one here. At school!"

Julie's eyes narrowed. "Do you hear them too? Like, are you hearing voices, Natalie?"

I think it was right then that my mom realized she shouldn't have said anything to Julie. Her cheeks flamed bright red and she blinked several times. It looked like she was trying to keep from crying.

"You know what, let's just forget about it," my mom said finally.

"I think that's the smartest thing you've said," Julie said emphatically. "I mean, no offense or anything, but you really shouldn't say stuff like that, Natalie. People will think you're crazy." Her voice dropped when she said the word "crazy."

Intense dislike for Julie shot through my body.

My mom just nodded miserably.

"Bell's going to ring. I need to go check my makeup," said Julie, jumping off the swing. "See you in math!"

The vision ended.

Two visions back to back had made me feel queasy. Not the throw-up kind, just the carsick kind. I felt as though I'd just spun around and around in a circle and then sat down. And I think what I'd seen in the last vision wasn't helping.

Why had my mom chosen to confide in someone like Julie? And why did she have such bad taste in friends? If only she had talked to Lady Azura first.

I stared back down at the diary, open to the page I'd left off. My mother's usually neat, round handwriting went all slanted and got a little messier. The next entry was about how Julie was acting weird. Ignoring her. Blowing her off to hang out with some girl named Tabitha instead. This is how the entry ended:

Julie thinks I'm crazy, and it's all my fault. Actually, it's Lady Azura's fault. All of this is probably

happening because of her. I am going to grow up to be
a big freak. I wish I had been born normal. This is all
so unfair!

There was that word again. Freak.

Had I ever felt like a freak? I know I used to wish I was normal. Like everyone else. But that was before I learned about my powers. Learned they were a gift. I was proud to be like Lady Azura. Proud to be related to her. My mother was being really unfair.

I closed the diary and sighed heavily. I felt so let down by my mother. Why couldn't she stand up for herself? Why would she want to even bother to remain friends with someone like Julie? There must have been great girls at school that my mom could have been friends with. Girls like Lily. Girls who knew how to be good friends. Girls who deserved your trust.

Thinking of Lily made me remember the hurt look she'd given me today as I left her. She needed my help, and so far I wasn't helping her. But the séance would change all that. I hadn't told her about it yet, just in case it didn't help. I didn't want to get her hopes up. But deep down, I had a feeling it was going to help.

I looked at the clock. Close to ten. I was sound asleep within ten minutes.

Chapter 10

At school on Monday I barely had a chance to talk with Lily alone. I managed to find her just before lunch. I asked her if she wanted to go to the construction site after school, but she told me she had to get home to watch Cammie while her mother took her brothers to buy soccer cleats.

Just before last period, I slammed my locker door closed and found myself staring at the spirit of Barkus, the old gym teacher who haunted the school. Usually I made a point of avoiding him. But just recently I'd finally caved and listened to what he had been trying to ask me.

"Collins," he said gruffly.

I sighed. Stopped. "Hi, Mr. Barkus," I said. "I have to hustle to math class."

"Thanks again for what you did. I owe ya one," he said.

"It was nothing," I said. All I'd done was go see an old lady who was in a nursing home. Decades ago, she and Barkus had been secretly in love with each other. He had asked me to tell her that he had always loved her, but that he'd died in a car accident before he'd gotten up the courage to tell her.

He shimmered away. And once again, I found myself staring at Jody Jenner.

She didn't say anything. Just cocked one eyebrow in my direction, turned, and headed away.

I sighed to myself. Why did she always have to be there to witness me talking to spirits? I used to be so careful about it at school. I had let my guard down way too much. I had to work on that. It was almost as if because I knew that Mason and Lily knew, I didn't care who else found out. But that wasn't totally true . . . it would lead to all sorts of questions if all the kids at school found out what I could do. And some of it is really private. I mean, I shouldn't have to explain it to everyone. Answer all the questions about it.

But that was different from being ashamed or embarrassed.

I smiled as I thought about it. I honestly didn't

care so much what the people thought anymore. It felt really good to know that.

When I got home from school, I could see that Lady Azura had a client. A strange car was in the driveway, and the purple curtain was pulled across the doorway to her séance room. I didn't feel like reading more in the diary. *Maybe I should start my own diary,* I thought.

But the thought of doing all that writing didn't really appeal to me. I'm a visual person. Maybe, I thought, I'd keep a visual diary. I raced upstairs to grab my camera, then headed back outside and wheeled my bike out of the shed.

I'd start by taking pictures of places around town that my mom might have gone to. When we'd first arrived here from California, my dad had shown me where she and her mom had once lived, although the house was no longer there. I wanted to see it again anyway. I pulled on my helmet and turned right out of the driveway, toward the road leading out of town.

What had once been rural farmland was now bustling development. The house where my mother and grandmother had lived for one year, before moving to Connecticut, was now a big warehouse store. I sighed and turned off the now-busy road, heading north, parallel to the boardwalk and the ocean. The busy strip almost immediately became a quiet residential street with modest houses. These had been built more recently than the older Victorians in our neighborhood. Another half mile, and the houses looked older. Farther apart. More like farmhouses. I stopped now and then to snap a picture of a pretty maple tree with colorful leaves, an old church, a weather-beaten clapboard house that looked like it had been built two hundred years ago.

I came to Culver Street and stopped for a moment before turning down it. This was the street where Lily's father wanted to buy the vacant lot. Half a mile down on the right, I came upon the lot. I stopped again. Stared at the place thoughtfully.

It looked harmless enough. Beach Drive lay ahead, and I could see the ocean from here. The lot itself wasn't as big as I had been expecting it to be. There wasn't much there. Clumps of sea grass and sandy mounds. A faded sign that said PRIVATE PROPERTY.

Toward the back of the lot, I saw a stack of old lumber, partly obscured by tall sea grass. Hadn't Lady Azura said this was the site of an old train depot? There was nothing left of that now. I got off my bike and laid it down on the edge of the lot. I walked across it, toward the battered, three-rail wooden fence separating the lot from the one on the other side, which was the back side of the supermarket.

Now I could make out the remains of old rails, grown over by grass and hidden by sand. And looking to my left, heading away from the ocean, I could see them more distinctly. Abandoned old rails to nowhere. Signs of an age when trains, rather than cars, moved people and cargo. I snapped some pictures.

Then the air shimmered. A mist passed across my vision. When it cleared, I saw five young men sitting on the fence, just a few feet down from where I was standing. Like workers on lunch break or something. But these were definitely spirits.

I stared. Blinked a few times. They shimmered, grew transparent, and disappeared. "Wait," I called. I wanted to tell them to come back and talk to me. But they were gone.

I'd only gotten a quick look, but I recognized the red-haired guy, the darker-skinned guy, and the one with the beret.

I got back onto my bike. These spirits were definitely connected to this land. This proved it.

When I arrived home, Lady Azura was still in with the client. I waited impatiently in the kitchen for a little while, eager for her to finish up so we could have our séance. But after a few more minutes I decided to go upstairs and read more of the diary.

Thursday, September 6
You'll never believe what happened today. My mom came home. She's furious with Lady Azura.

The page swam in front of me. I was having another vision. I swallowed hard, feeling rising nausea. So many visions. They were taking a lot out of me, I realized. I'd had visions before but never so many, so fast.

I was standing in a kitchen. An unfamiliar one. Smaller than Lady Azura's. Painted a cheerful light blue, with a black-and-white tiled floor. My mom was sitting at the table, her chin in her hands, her long, straight hair cascading over her shoulders. Standing near her was—shocker—a younger version of Lady Azura. There was no mistaking her, though. Same dyed mahogany hair. Same exotic clothing. Same glamorously made-up face. But she looked twenty-five years younger. She was stunning.

Next to Lady Azura was another woman. It had to be my grandmother, Diana, whom I had never met. She was also startlingly pretty, though in a much simpler way than Lady Azura. She barely wore any makeup, and her hair was back in a twist. She had dark eyes like Lady Azura. My mom must have gotten her blue eyes from her father.

"Mom! What are you doing home so soon?" my mom asked. "I thought you weren't due back until this weekend."

"Julie's mother called me," replied Diana, her voice guarded. She looked from my mother to Lady Azura and then back at my mother.

My mom gulped, and her face got very pale.

My heart sank. So Julie had run home and told her mother what my mom had told her. And her mom had called Diana and told her everything, and

Diana had come running home.

My mom looked scared. She tap-tap-tapped the eraser on the table. It was the loudest sound in the kitchen.

"Go upstairs now, Nat. I need to talk to your grandmother alone."

Lady Azura's lips were pressed together in what I knew was a defiant way. Her arms were crossed in front of her.

My mom slid from her chair and headed out of the kitchen. But as I looked after her, the walls turned shimmery and transparent. I could see that she stopped just on the other side of the door and stayed to listen. She'd taken the pencil with her. The eraser end was now at her mouth, and I could see her tapping it against her front teeth.

"Mom," said Diana, after she was sure that my mom was out of earshot, which of course, she wasn't. "What is going on? Mary Kane called me. Julie's mother. She told me that Julie had told her that Natalie is nattering on to Julie about paranormal phenomenon, how she can see ghosts. What kind of nonsense have you been feeding her?"

My mom took the pencil away from her mouth. I watched her snap it in half.

Lady Azura's eyes flashed. "I've had no such talks with Natalie," she said. "I would of course have been more than happy to discuss it if she had approached me, but she did not. I was not aware that Natalie possessed any powers. Were you aware of this before now?"

"She doesn't have any powers," snapped Diana. "I knew it was a mistake to leave for so long. Clearly this is a cry for help from Natalie."

Lady Azura looked hurt, or at least I think she did. My heart ached for her. This wasn't her fault. Diana was being harsh toward her. But I could only watch and listen.

"I think I should take that job in Connecticut," said Diana. Her face softened a little as she noticed the hurt look on her mother's face. "I really appreciate all you've done for us, Mom. Truly I do. It's just that I think Natalie needs some stability. Some normalcy in her life. I'm going upstairs to talk with her."

The bits of pencil flew out of my mom's hands as she rushed across the room and tiptoed hurriedly up the stairs. I followed Diana out of the kitchen door and traipsed up the stairs behind her, into a bedroom at the top of the stairs.

Interested as I was in hearing the conversation unfold, I was also fascinated to be standing in my mother's bedroom. It looked so different from mine. Just like the blue bedroom where my mom had been staying at Lady Azura's, this room was a mess. Piles of stuff were strewn around. Shoes, draped clothing, open dresser drawers. The walls were white, and the furnishings pretty plain, but then, I realized, it was most likely a rented house. They wouldn't have painted it for just a one-year stay. But there was artwork stuck up all over. Pastels, watercolors, charcoals, landscapes, figures, fantasy scenes.

I focused on the conversation in front of me. Diana was speaking to my mom. Lady Azura had followed her up the stairs and was standing at the door of the room. This was really weird to see, as Lady Azura never climbed stairs anymore.

"Natalie, honey," said Diana in a soothing voice. She crossed the room and sat down on my mom's bed. My mom sat with her knees up, her arms clasped around them, her shoulders slightly hunched, like she was bracing herself for something.

"Julie has told her mother that you said you were seeing things. Hearing people speak. Paranormal things. Is that true?"

There followed a long silence. The clock ticked. The tension in the room was palpable. At last my mom spoke.

"Um, well, I might have said something along those lines to Julie," my mom said as if she was struggling to remember. "But I was, um, just kidding around. Like, no big deal."

"Could this be the result of spending so much time with your grandmother?" asked Diana.

"Now just a minute—" began Lady Azura indignantly, but Diana interrupted her.

"Maybe just hearing her talk about it so much has put these ideas into your head?" prompted Diana. "Wishful thinking or something?"

"Um, yes!" said my mom, looking relieved. "That's totally it. I must have just been listening to Lady Azura talking about it so much that I just thought it sounded cool. That's probably what happened. Because really,

I was just kidding. I don't see ghosts. Or hear them. That would be totally weird and awful, right, Mom?"

The hard, tense lines in Diana's face softened. My mother had told her just what she had wanted to hear.

But Lady Azura's face fell. She looked so disappointed. I wanted to rush across the room and hug her, but of course I couldn't. I turned to look at my mother. She was avoiding looking at Lady Azura. She must have felt terrible.

You should feel terrible, I wanted to tell my mother. I couldn't believe the way she had hurt Lady Azura.

The vision ended.

I sat there holding the diary, feeling betrayed by my own mother.

I scanned the rest of the entry. I read how Diana had asked Lady Azura to leave. How my mom felt really badly about all of it, but blamed her "stupid powers" as she had begun calling them, for everything. How if she could have one wish, just one, it would be more than anything that she could make these powers go away.

I closed the book.

Chapter 11

I woke up early Tuesday morning. I was still tired, but I couldn't sleep anymore—probably because I had fallen asleep so early. After putting the diary away, I'd gone downstairs and had a quiet dinner of leftover soup with my dad. He and I shared a turkey sandwich along with the soup. My dad looked like he'd had a long day too.

Lady Azura's client had stayed past eight p.m., and when I saw how tired she looked, I didn't have the heart to ask her if we could do our séance. There was still plenty of time, I told myself. Plus, I knew my heart wouldn't have been in it. I was too upset about my mom.

I had done a lot of tossing and turning all night, thinking about my mother. How disappointed I felt. Wondering why she'd even wanted me to look at this diary. Why she'd bothered to send Duggan to tell me where to find it. Was she trying to tell me how to get rid of my own powers? Maybe that's why her spirit had never appeared for me.

Maybe she didn't want me to see her. Didn't even want me to be able to.

I pulled out the diary from beneath my bed, where I'd stashed it the night before. Opened it to the entry I'd left off at.

Friday, September 7

I'm ashamed of what I did, Diary. But I have to live my life, right? All I want is to be normal. To have these spirits go away and stop bothering me. I hate these stupid powers. My grandmother is probably upset with me, and I don't blame her. But she likes seeing spirits. I don't. Not one bit. I wish with all my heart that I could make them stop.

Several days passed without another entry. And then I read this.

Wednesday, September 19

Sorry I've been away for so long, Diary. But the

best thing has happened! My powers are gone! I think for good! It's been almost a week since I had an "encounter." And yesterday I rode my bike over to Lady Azura's house, even though Mom says I am not allowed to go over there since their big fight. But I wanted to test it out. Usually when I'm over there, that's when I have the most problems. But yesterday I didn't see one single spirit or hear any weird voices. Hooray!

My grandmother asked me all kinds of questions about my mom. She seems really upset about the fight. I feel bad that I kind of caused the fight. But she was really nice to me. I think she's as convinced as my mom is that I made it all up just to get attention. That I was never able to really see spirits. That's fine with me if that's what she thinks. She did ask me to promise to tell her if I ever start seeing spirits so we could talk about it together. I promised, but I had my fingers crossed behind my back. Hopefully my powers are gone for good, though!

I decided I'd read enough.

I closed the book, got out of bed, and opened my

closet. Standing on tiptoes, I shoved it way up on the highest shelf, behind a pair of old boots that didn't fit. I wasn't going to read it anymore. I felt no connection at all to my mom. I didn't want anything more to do with the book. It just made me feel worse. But at least it explained why Lady Azura had told me that my mother did not possess any powers.

As I walked into school later that morning, I felt my ruby crystal vibrating again. Was it trying to tell me something about Mason? Maybe I should make more of an effort than I'd been making.

I found Mason trying to cram his sports bag into his locker. He was jamming it in with his foot. It looked like he'd have a tough time getting the door to close on it.

"Hey," I said, turning to lean against the row of lockers next to his and staring down with amusement as he tried to readjust the bag.

"Stupid bag," he mumbled. "Hey yourself."

"So, how've you been? It's been a while since I've seen you."

Mason screwed up his face and looked adorably puzzled. "Didn't I see you on Sunday at the arcade?"

"Oh, right!" I laughed. I was making a mess of this. I decided to just plunge right in. "So listen, do you want to try and go out again? Since our get-together got kind of—cut short?"

He turned to me. "Yeah, sure," he said. "Maybe we can stay away from the crowds this time. Maybe this coming Saturday. We could go for pizza in Harbor Isle. But, um, maybe we shouldn't make a big deal of it at school. Like, just pretend we're not, like, a couple."

I blinked at him, not sure what he meant. "Okay. Why?"

He shrugged. "Just because, well, I don't know. You and I, we, um, give off a lot of energy when we're in the same place at the same time. I think other people sense it. Me with my, you know, and you with your, you know. You know?"

I didn't really know. But I guessed he meant the fact that he had powers and so did I. That somehow that wasn't a good combination. I opened my mouth and then closed it again, not sure what to say.

The bell rang.

"Got to get to class," I said. "Good luck with that bag."

I headed off. I didn't feel great about our

conversation. Why would we need to pretend? It seemed wrong somehow. Was I misunderstanding what he had meant?

Just before lunch, Mason flagged me down near the water fountain outside the cafeteria.

"What's up?" I asked him. "Are you sure this is wise? I thought we weren't supposed to be seen talking together," I added teasingly. I hoped he would tell me I was being silly, that I had misunderstood what he meant before.

He didn't.

"Listen, um, I was in study hall with a group of kids last period, and Jody was talking about you."

I swallowed. "What was she saying?"

"Well . . ." He looked right and left, then down, like he couldn't meet my eye. "She said she thinks you think you hear voices. That you're, you know." He twisted a finger around in a circle near his head, as if to describe a crazy person.

I stared at him. I could feel hot tears behind my eyes, but I forced them back. They weren't tears of humiliation. They were tears of anger. At Jody. And also a little at Mason. I had a feeling he hadn't jumped to my defense. Although I couldn't be sure. I thought of my mom and lifted my chin. "Well, I can't really control what other people say about me, Mason."

"Yeah, well, but there's a little more to it. Everyone kind of looked at me, like to see if I knew all about it. I just changed the subject. But a lot of people seem to know we were out together Saturday night. Jody and her friends." He shrugged. "I just thought you should know that everyone knows we hung out or whatever."

I crossed my arms. Forget angry. Now I was just confused. "Well, what does that matter? We *were* out together, weren't we?"

"It's just, I don't like being talked about," he said. "What if they find out about your, you know, powers? And what if they somehow find out about mine? That would just be so uncool."

"Okay," I said. I didn't see what the big deal was. "I'll be more careful from now on. It was a really unfortunate coincidence that Jody happened to pop out of nowhere the two times I happened to say something to a spirit." It was actually three times. Twice with Barkus, and once with the spirit on the boardwalk. But I didn't think it would help my case to share every detail.

The bell rang for lunch, and we headed into the cafeteria. I couldn't help but notice that he fell back a step, walking behind me, as though to signal that we were not together.

Mason and I sat at separate tables, as we usually did. As I set down my tray at the table with Lily and Marlee and Miranda and several girls from Harbor Isle, Jody was in the middle of talking about her father's new commercial. Everyone else at the table was listening raptly, except Lily, who was doing her best to look bored.

I sat down. Quietly picked up my fork and poked my mac and cheese as I listened to the conversation.

"So yeah, it's just a commercial, a twenty-second spot, but still. I can't believe I get to be in it!"

"Awesome," breathed Miranda.

"I'm lip-synching the music, of course. It's a commercial for breath mints." Jody giggled, and everyone at the table laughed except me and Lily. I took a sip of milk and shot Lily a look. She shot back an almost-imperceptible eye roll.

"So what do you have to do?" asked Marlee.

"I pretend to be singing about how great the mints are, and then I pop one in my mouth"—she popped an imaginary breath mint into her mouth, then tossed back her glossy hair and smiled confidently—"and then I go striding up to this hot guy and lean in close to him— you know, because I'm so confident my breath is minty fresh—and I say something to him and laugh, and he laughs back." She pantomimed the dramatic swaggering walk, even though she was sitting down.

Several girls laughed. The rest of the table seemed struck dumb with awe.

"And then they cut to a shot of the breath mint and a guy voices over how great they are and that's that. But here's the best part. Guess who's going to play the hot guy? Don't tell them, Sara or Caroline!"

"Who?" asked everyone at the table except me and Lily and Caroline. Lily and I were the only ones not leaning forward toward the center of the table. Caroline looked ecstatic to be in on the secret already.

"Mason Meyer! I know, right? He said yes, although his buddies are giving him a lot of grief about it." She giggled.

All eyes swiveled to look at me. One of Lily's eye-brows cocked upward with surprise.

I shrugged like it was interesting and smiled so as not to appear rude, but I wasn't going to pretend I thought it was a big deal. Because it wasn't.

I realized right then and there that I really didn't care one way or the other.

Chapter 12

That afternoon I asked Lily if she wanted to walk by the vacant lot, but she had to stay after school to finish a project. I took the long way home, taking a few more pictures for my journal. Many of the stores on the boardwalk, I knew, hadn't changed since my mom's day. As I walked, I thought about what my mother had written in that last entry. How her powers seemed to have vanished. How could that be? Could she just have willed them to go away? I could ask Lady Azura. But I wasn't yet ready to tell her about the diary.

As I turned into our driveway, a car I didn't know was just pulling out. I guessed it was a client of Lady Azura's.

I found her in the sitting room off the front hall, sprawled in the armchair near the fireplace.

"Everything okay?" I asked her anxiously. "You look tired."

"I am, my dear," she admitted, passing a hand across her brow. "I had a long and difficult session with a client just now. A man and his late brother, long estranged, endeavoring to communicate with each other. It was difficult enough for them to communicate with each other in this world, which made it doubly difficult with one of them in the next. I feel a cup of tea is in order. And then a nice long nap."

I offered to put the kettle on for her. It didn't seem right to bring up the idea of doing the séance for the young-man spirits I'd been seeing. She seemed weary enough as it was.

Lady Azura joined me in the kitchen as I was pouring the hot water into her teacup for her. I knew just how she liked it, of course. I set down the sugar bowl and watched with amusement as she began the elaborate process of adding cream and sugar to her cup.

"May I ask you something?" I asked her, as she stirred the cup contentedly.

"You may always ask me something, my dear," she said with a smile.

"How is it possible for someone to make their powers go away?" I asked, thinking of my mother. "I mean, is it possible? Can you have them, and then wish for them to vanish and they do?"

A troubled look appeared on her face. "Sara, I thought you had gotten to a place where you embraced your powers. Are you reaching a point where you would wish them away?"

"Oh, no," I said quickly. "I don't mean for me. I love having powers. I would never in a zillion years wish them away. It's part of who I am. "

An amused look played across her face.

"What?" I asked. The way she was looking at me was making me feel embarrassed. "What?" I demanded again.

Lady Azura grinned and reached over to squeeze my hand. "It's just that you have changed so much. Grown so much. It wasn't that long ago that you would have wished your powers away if you could have."

I started to protest, but she kept talking. "When you first came here, you were so confused. So desperate to be 'normal.' Don't you remember?"

I clamped my mouth shut and stared at her. She was right, of course. I'd forgotten.

"Did I really hate my powers that much? I guess I'm a completely different person than I was last year."

"Change is a natural part of life, Sara," Lady Azura said, nodding. "Especially at your age. Why, when I was a young girl like you, I was practically a different person from year to year. You are far more grounded—far more mature—than most young girls. But you have come a very long way in a very short time."

I reflected. I guessed she was right. I *had* come a long way. And it was almost all because of Lady Azura. I wished so much that my mother had been able to get this same guidance from Lady Azura almost thirty years ago. Would things have turned out differently? I wondered.

Then I thought of Mason. He seemed so ashamed of his powers. I felt sorry for him. He didn't have Lady Azura in his life either. I didn't know if he had anyone who could really help him the way she had helped me.

I was so incredibly lucky.

That evening my dad made spaghetti and meat-balls. The three of us had a quiet dinner together. After the dishes, I did homework and then went to bed. I'd lost interest in the diary. I took off my necklace because my ruby crystal was buzzing like a telephone set to vibrate.

Chapter 13

The next day, Wednesday, was dull and rainy.

At school I learned within the first two seconds of arriving that the commercial shoot had happened the previous afternoon. It felt like the whole school was buzzing about it. All my friends had been invited to go watch, except me. And Lily, of course. But she wouldn't have been able to go anyway, since I knew she'd been working on a project.

I found myself avoiding Mason, but I'm not sure he even noticed, because the three times during the day that I saw him he was surrounded by groups of kids. All talking about the commercial.

I found myself avoiding Lily, too. I couldn't wait to go home and do the séance after school with Lady Azura. Until I had something helpful to tell Lily, I didn't want to see her and have her ask me for my advice again.

If I was going to give her advice, I wanted it to be great advice. Lily deserved that.

Wednesday afternoon I ran straight home from school and went in search of Lady Azura. I found her in her séance room, but she didn't have a client. She was tidying up, replacing old candles and stuff, but stopped what she was doing, looking genuinely happy to see me.

"Are you available for that séance?" I asked her after we'd exchanged news about our days.

"I was going to suggest the same thing," she said. "My last client had to cancel, so I'm free the rest of the afternoon."

This was a rare event, having her free. When we first moved here, her clients had been few and far between. But last spring she'd been featured in some news stories after she'd helped Mason's family recover some missing jewelry, and her business had been booming ever since.

I followed her into the séance room.

The room faced east, so the late afternoon light that came in through the partly open, heavy drapes cast long shadows across the room.

She lit two candles on the side credenza and then pointed to the chair at the table she expected me to sit at. She walked over to the table and arranged some crystals in the center. The light from the flickering candles made them sparkle. Then she sat down across the table from me. She took both my hands in hers.

She put her chin down and began speaking in a low, velvety voice.

"We are here, my great-granddaughter and I," she began. "We want to hear from you, the young men who have been trying to talk to Sara. We want to know what it is you are trying to tell her." Her eyes were closed, her thick, dark lashes—which I knew were glued on because I'd seen her without her "face" on—contrasting with the crepe-papery, powdery-white skin of her face. The heady scent of the candles made me feel drowsy.

I closed my eyes too. Opened my mind the way Lady Azura had taught me to. Tried to relax every muscle. Asked them to come to us. Invited their presence.

It's hard to explain exactly how you conjure someone. For a long time, I struggled with it. I used to ask Lady Azura to tell me exactly what to do, and she would tell me to just close my eyes and focus. I used to do that and nothing happened. But now I was getting really good at it. I felt the air thicken around me, and I knew they were here with us.

I opened my eyes.

I saw the five shadowy figures standing behind Lady Azura. Five young men, two taller, two of medium build, the fifth short but powerfully built. I recognized them. The taller ones were the young man in the red beret I'd seen that day outside Scoops and the dark-skinned young man—still a boy, really—I'd seen at the boardwalk. And then there was a red-haired boy, and two others, both of whom I was pretty sure I had seen before, sitting on the fence at the vacant lot. Each had a cap he had taken off his head and held in his hands.

Lady Azura's eyes opened. She looked at me. Saw me looking over her shoulder and turned slowly.

"Can you see them?" I whispered to her as quietly as I could. I knew she couldn't always see spirits the way I could.

"I can sense that they are there," she whispered back. "But you must speak, Sara. They are here because of you. It's you they want to talk to."

I cleared my throat and asked them if they had something they wanted to tell me.

The red-haired young man in the middle seemed to be the spokesman for the group. He took a little step forward. Then he spoke.

"If you please, miss," he said. "You must ask 'im to cease and desist."

"I—I'll try," I said. "But who am I supposed to ask? I am not sure what you want me to do."

"The gentleman who was there, 'im as was walking about," he said.

The dark-skinned boy cleared his throat. "The one as drives the horseless carriage, miss. The green one."

"Oh!" I said. "You mean Lily's dad. Mr. Randazzo? Tall and muscular with dark hair?"

They exchanged looks with one another as though wanting to come to a consensus. All of them then looked at me and nodded.

"Did something—happen to you there?" I asked.

More looking at one another for support. More nodding in unison.

I waited. I'd learned when dealing with spirits that

sometimes letting them direct the conversation got better results than trying to ask specific questions.

"We was subcontracted by the Pennsylvania-Jersey Coastal Lines to build the new depot in Stellamar," said the short one. "It was a grand design."

The red-haired guy spoke up. "I did the masonry on the corbelled chimney."

The darker-skinned boy added, "I had just begun to lay the slate roof. 'Twas to have half-timbering and stucco walls, iron ridge cresting, decorative stick work in the gables, and carved brackets supporting its broad eaves. . . ."

I waited, wondering what had happened.

"'Twas a cave-in," said the spokesman finally.

"In aught eight," added another.

The spokesman went on. "An old conduit—wooden, of course—laid a century before, and paved over. 'Twas an explosion and a cave-in. We five were there. A dozen more perished as well. Only two of our original crew survived."

"I'm so sorry," I said. And I was. They looked so young.

"But miss," said the short one. "You must warn

the gentleman he must dig beneath the later pip-
ing, nearly to the bedrock. The old conduits must be
removed."

"Or another cave-in is certain," said the spokesman.

"Is that—is that why no one has been able to
build there?" I asked as the pieces all fell together
around me. "Have you been—protecting people from
the certainty of another cave-in?"

All five nodded.

"Thank you," I said. "I'll do what I can."

They shimmered out of view, all five of them looking immensely relieved.

"I believe I heard the gist of it," Lady Azura said
a moment later. "They were the construction workers, then?"

I nodded. Filled her in on the details of the conversation. Then I asked her what I should do.

"You must tell Lily, and find a way to tell her
father," said Lady Azura simply.

"But he'll never believe it," I protested. "I can't tell
him I was visited by a bunch of spirits. He would never
believe something as wild and far-fetched as this. How
am I ever going to convince him?"

"I trust you will find a way, Sara," she said as she smiled at me. "You can be very resourceful."

I texted Lily as soon as I was out of the séance room.

CAN I COME OVER TO CU? IT'S IMPORTANT.

A couple of hours went by before she responded.

SORRY. I HAD TO TAKE MY BROTHERS TO THE LIBRARY. AT AUNT ANGELA'S FOR DINNER. AND YOU KNOW HER NO-TEXTING RULE. HAD TO DO THIS IN THE BATHROOM!

My phone buzzed as a second text came in from Lily.

WILL GET HOME TOO LATE TONIGHT, BUT DO YOU WANT TO SLEEP OVER FRIDAY NIGHT? WE HAVE MUCHO TO CATCH UP ON!

I smiled as I texted back, saying that of course I wanted to sleep over Friday night. I didn't really want to wait so long to tell her what the construction workers had told me, but then again, there was still plenty of time before her dad signed any of the paperwork.

I knew that Lily and I would be able to think of some way to convince her dad not to go through with the deal. It felt really good to know I was going to be able to help my best friend.

Chapter 14

It rained all day on Thursday, too, but luckily, the day flew by. I managed to avoid Mason at school. It was getting really easy to do. I think maybe he was avoiding me, too.

Friday afternoon Lily and I walked home from school together. I stopped by my house to drop off my backpack and grab my overnight stuff, and then headed right back over to her house. Lily's mom and dad were out with the guy Lily's dad was thinking about entering into the business deal with.

"Yeah, about that," I told Lily. "I have some info I need to share with you about it. Lady Azura and I did a séance, and I learned some stuff—"

"What's a say-ons?" asked Cammie, Lily's little sister.

Lily's eyes got wide, and I clapped my hand over my mouth. I hadn't realized Cammie was within earshot, but it made sense she would be. She practically glued herself to my side whenever I was there.

"A séance is what Lady Azura does sometimes," Lily explained simply. "How about if we go outside and play for a while?"

And just like that, Cammie forgot all about it. By unspoken agreement, I knew Lily and I would talk about it later, after Cammie was in bed.

We played outside with Lily's brothers, Cammie, and Buddy the dog until it was time for dinner. Then we made them grilled-cheese-and-tomato sandwiches and broccoli and carrot sticks. Fed Buddy. Got Cammie into and out of the bath. Cammie demanded that I read to her, so I headed up to her room and snuggled on her bed with her and read her a bunch of books while the boys watched a movie.

At last Cammie was in bed with her stuffed frog and the light out—but the door slightly open—and the boys were upstairs playing quietly in their room. I could talk to Lily in private.

We went into the kitchen and made some hot chocolate. As I stirred it, I told her about the séance. About the spirits I'd seen.

Lily's brown eyes got wider. "So the place really *is* jinxed!" she said.

"Well, I don't think I'd call it jinxed exactly," I said. "'Jinxed' sounds so negative, and the spirits have been trying to help prevent people from getting hurt, so they mean well. They seem sure that another cave-in is extremely likely because of those crumbling old pipes buried way deep down, below where most normal developers would dig. So you have to make your dad know about those pipes somehow."

She pulled her ponytail and absently twirled it around her fingers, a gesture I knew meant she was deep in thought. "He won't believe us if we tell him about the spirits," she said. "As soon as we start to tell him that we learned all this from a bunch of spirits, he'll stop listening and won't take us seriously."

"I know," I said. "I've been thinking a lot about it, and I have an idea. What if we research the accident? There has to be something in an old newspaper or something. We can find proof of what happened there and share it with him. That way we can maybe convince him without ever mentioning the spirits."

Lily's face lit up. "Yes! That's a *great* idea, Sar!" she said, leaping to her feet. "And I know just where to start—at the visitors' information center on the board-walk. Great-Aunt Ro still works there on the weekends. We can go see her in the morning and ask her how to find out about what happened."

Lily's great-aunt Ro had helped me out once before, though she didn't know it. The summer I first moved to Stellamar, I was being visited by a ghost who needed me to help him prevent a trag-edy on the boardwalk. I was too afraid to listen to him, let alone help him, until I found out from Great-Aunt Ro who he had been in life. He'd been a really good, kind man who loved kids and was always helping people. Once I knew that, I was able to give his spirit a chance. I'm so glad I did, because together we prevented a fire.

We spent the next hour getting Lily's brothers to bed and tidying up the kitchen. Mr. and Mrs. Randazzo came home as we were heading up to bed ourselves.

"Hi, Sara," said Mrs. Randazzo, giving me a quick hug. "Thanks for helping Lily out tonight."

She looked tired to me. Mr. Randazzo wasn't his

usual cheerful self either. He excused himself and went into the study to check his e-mail. Lily and I exchanged a look and went upstairs.

"So much stress," she said under her breath to me as we brushed our teeth side by side in the double sinks of the upstairs bathroom. "They're never like this."

"We'll help them work it out," I said as reassuringly as I could.

Lily had one of those cool beds that has a second bed under it that can be pulled out. It was already all set up for me. Tonight I would be sleeping on Cinderella sheets that I had a feeling belonged to Cammie.

After we turned out the light, talk turned to boys.

"So how much do you care that Jody is spending every waking second with Mason?" asked Lily. "Does that bother you?"

"Weirdly, no," I said. "I really do think I'm changing my mind about Mason. I was so excited when he asked me out, but when we went out together, I didn't have the greatest time."

"But wasn't that all Jody's fault?" Lily asked.

"Well, we didn't have to sit with her. Mason *wanted*

to, I think. And I could have said no. We could have told her we were out together and sat by ourselves. But we didn't do that. And besides, I wasn't having very much fun before we bumped into Jody anyway."

"I think you're way too nice," Lily said. But then she added quickly, "Though I do see your point. And you're right. Especially if it wasn't fun even before you bumped into Miss Minty-Fresh Breath."

I laughed a little at Lily's new nickname for Jody. "I don't know, Lil," I said a moment later. "It's not like it was with Jayden. I never had to think about what to say, topics to discuss, when I was with him. With Mason, things feel forced. It's kind of stressful."

I couldn't tell Lily the other reason I was bothered. That Mason was so embarrassed by his powers. And that he probably wasn't okay with mine, either, which made me feel like he wasn't okay with who I was.

"So how are you going to deal with it?" asked Lily. "Just break up with him?"

I shrugged. "We're not even really officially going out. So I'd feel pretty dumb saying I want to break up. I guess I'll just avoid him. Which hasn't been very hard to do, so that should tell you something. We're supposed to have another 'date'"—I said this in air quotes, even though I knew Lily couldn't see me in the dark—"to go for pizza in Harbor Isle tomorrow night, but I might just text him and cancel."

"Yeah, just cancel on him," Lily agreed. "I'm pretty much over Cal, too," she added with a heavy sigh. "I don't know what I saw in him. Maybe just because he was new, and I was sick of all the boys at Stellamar. But we have nothing—zip—nada—in common. And he's really kind of boring! What on earth was I thinking?"

We giggled and then that dissolved into a huge laughing fit. I don't know why it was so funny that Lily had declared Cal boring, but it was somehow hilarious. We finally stopped laughing when Lily reminded me, between giggles, that we had to keep quiet or else we'd wake up her parents.

Before we fell asleep, we vowed to only crush on boys in the future that we thought were worthy of us.

We woke up pretty early Saturday morning. We dressed quickly, ate quickly, and were out the door and heading toward the visitors' information center just a few minutes before nine.

Great-Aunt Ro was just opening up.

"Well! This is a pleasant surprise!" she exclaimed upon seeing Lily. She greeted me warmly too.

"Hey, Great-Aunt Ro," said Lily, giving her a quick hug. "So Sara and I are here to research something."

"Oh! For a school project?" she asked.

Lily and I exchanged a look. We hadn't really discussed ahead of time what our reason for researching would be. But before we could think of how to answer, Great-Aunt Ro went on talking.

"I'm so happy to have a task to keep me busy. It's such a slow time of year, now that the tourists have all left," she said. "So what are we researching?"

I had written down the name of the railroad that the young man had mentioned in the séance. I pulled out the piece of paper and read it. "We're doing research on the railroads. Wasn't there a Pennsylvania-Jersey Coastal Line running through the town a hundred years or so ago?"

Great-Aunt Ro's face furrowed into a frown, thinking. "Hmm," she said. "I know that there used to be a railroad that ran through town here. Some of it is still in operation by the commuter train, but not here in

Stellamar. I believe the Harbor Isle stop is the nearest one. But yes, there was definitely a track running through town. Just where, though, I can't say." She massaged her chin thoughtfully.

"Can we look it up somewhere?" asked Lily.

"You most certainly can," said Great-Aunt Ro. "We have the *Stellamar Sentinel* on microfilm in the basement."

"What's microfilm?" we both asked at the same time.

Great-Aunt Ro chuckled. "You kids. You have it so easy these days, with the Internet. But back in my college days, if you had to research something that happened a century ago, you had to look on microfilm. Come on. I'll show you how it works."

We followed her around the counter and then downstairs, into the basement. It smelled of musty furniture and old leather. Great-Aunt Ro sat Lily down in front of an antique-looking machine that looked a little like a huge computer from the eighties. I pulled up a chair next to Lily. Great-Aunt Ro opened a long, flat drawer, scanned down the line of small boxes, and pulled one out.

Inside was a miniature reel of film. She helped us

thread it into the machine, then flicked on the switch. The front page of a newspaper appeared.

"Whoa!" we both exclaimed.

"Well, I need to get back upstairs to man the fort," said Great-Aunt Ro after she demonstrated for us how to turn the spool so you could see the next page. "You girls have fun."

It was fun for about five minutes. We scanned the paper's headlines, giggled at some of the ads for corsets and horse harnesses and medical elixirs, and then realized how long it could take to find what we'd come for.

"We don't even know what year the cave-in happened," said Lily. She twirled the spool firmly, and dozens of pages streamed past. "We're only in 1900. What if it was 1920 or something? We'll be here all day."

I nodded grimly.

"Do you remember if anyone mentioned *when* it happened? Any clues at all?"

I closed my eyes.

Concentrated hard on remembering.

Suddenly my eyes flew open.

"Aught eight," I said.

"What?"

"Aught eight. That's what one of the spirits said."

"What ought to be eight?" asked Lily, looking confused.

"Not ought. Aught. A-U-G-H-T. It means zero in olden-day language."

"So . . . oh-eight." The realization dawned. "1908!" she said excitedly.

I nodded. We rewound the film, put it back in its box, and scanned the other boxes until we found the year 1908. I helped her thread the film in, the way we'd seen Great-Aunt Ro do it.

We found a front-page headline in January:

Modern Depot Planned for Stellamar Junction

Then, in May, we found another article about how digging of the foundation was to commence as soon as the ground was workable.

In June we read how workers under contract from the Pennsylvania-Jersey Coastal Lines were beginning work.

In late July we found this article. Lily and I read it in silence.

Stellamar Depot Site Explosion and Cave-In Engulfs a Score

Nearly twenty workers perish. Buried in tons of debris fifty feet down, while others slide into Death Pit.

Mayor Directs Recovery.

An explosion of gas shook the neighborhood as there was a cave-in at the construction site for the train depot on Culver Street yesterday morning, burying, it is believed, at least twenty persons fifty feet below the surface. A flood of water from broken mains added to the calamity.

Scores of firemen, policemen, and other municipal employees attempted rescue, but danger of further cave-in meant the impossibility of recovering the victims.

Experts believe that the old drains running beneath the mains created the deadly buildup of methane gas and led to the cave-in.

I stopped reading. "This is the evidence we need, Lil," I said. "We have to make a copy and show this article to your dad."

Lily rocked back and forth in her chair in excitement. "The article even mentions 'old drains.' If they were old back in 1908, then they must be *really* old now. My dad will totally pay attention to this!"

We managed to take a decent, readable picture with Lily's cell phone, which had better quality than mine. Then we packed everything away again, turned off the machine, and headed upstairs.

"Thanks so much, Great-Aunt Ro!" yelled Lily over her shoulder as we raced out of the front door.

Great-Aunt Ro was sitting on a low stool in front of the display case, restocking brochures. "You're welcome, girls!" she called after us. "Come back soon!"

We ran back to Lily's house, where we found her dad in the study, reading over a long, legal-looking document. His new reading glasses, which Lily had told me he'd finally decided he needed, were perched on his nose somewhat awkwardly. Like he wasn't quite used to wearing them yet.

"What's up, girls?" he said distractedly, without

looking up from his paper. "Kind of busy. Have to finish looking this over before I get it off to the lawyer."

"Wait! You mean you already signed the contract?" shrieked Lily. "I thought you weren't signing the paperwork for another couple of weeks!"

Lily's dad shot her a bewildered look, as if he didn't understand why it had upset her so much to learn he had signed the paperwork early. "Well, we moved ahead with it yesterday. Signed the paperwork right at dinner last night. Your mom and I talked about it, Lil, and we decided to just do it." He smiled as he said it, but he sounded a little tense. "There's nothing to worry about," he added.

"But Daddy, you have to look at this," said Lily, striding into the room. She looked as panicked as I felt. She set her phone down on top of the document.

"Lil, I don't have time to look at pictures or videos right now," he said, moving the phone off to the side. "Honey, I want to talk about whatever is bothering you, but can it just wait just a bit? I promise I'll be all ears soon. . . . I just need to run this over to my lawyer before he closes at noon."

"Dad, you have to listen to me!" Lily said firmly.

"This isn't about a problem I am having. This is about a problem *you* are going to have if you don't stop and look at what I am trying to tell you!"

Maybe it was the urgency in her voice, or maybe it was the fact that Lily had raised her voice to her father, something she would never ordinarily do. But she had his full attention now. He sat down in his chair and looked her in the eye.

"Tell me," he said, a worried frown appearing on his face.

So Lily and I told him what we'd discovered. Lily pointed to the article on her phone for emphasis, but we didn't even really need it. He listened as she explained what we had learned. How there were older pipes at the site he had just purchased, far below the later ones. How they had to be excavated before anything could be safely built there, otherwise there would be a risk of another cave-in. We of course didn't say anything about the spirits. We stuck to the facts. Lily presented everything in a calm, steady voice. I chimed in every now and then, but really Lily had it all under control.

I had never been so impressed with my best friend.

Mr. Randazzo sat back in his chair as he digested

everything he'd just heard. "Wow, girls, this is a nice piece of detective work. How in the world did you think to look this up?"

I had no idea how to answer that. Luckily, Lily spoke up.

"We were wondering why the place is supposed to be jinxed. We knew a lot of businesses had been attempted there and things just kept happening. We figured there had to be a logical explanation behind all the superstitious talk. So we did some investigating at the visitors' information center."

Lily's dad came around his desk and engulfed us both in a quick hug, one on each side of him. He was a big man, much bigger than my dad, and solid as an oak tree.

"I'm really grateful to you two," he said.

"But what are you going to do, Daddy?" Lily asked, her composure seeming to waver now that the story was out and her dad believed us. "You already signed the contract last night. Can you get your money back?"

Lily's dad looked pained to hear the worry in her voice. "It will be okay, sweetheart. The fact that I know all of this up front—before we began any work—is what really matters. I'll talk to Cousin Dominick. He can come out with his heavy equipment team. Seems like excavating down another fifteen feet should solve the problem. It's going to cost a lot. But he'll give me a good price, I'm sure."

Lily and I exchanged relieved looks.

Mr. Randazzo picked up Lily's phone again and reread the headline. "I'll have Ro make me a copy of this article," he said. "I'll bring copies of it to the zoning commission meeting. It makes me shudder to think I might have commenced construction without doing this. You girls have probably averted a potentially huge second disaster."

As Lily's dad strode out of the room, his phone in hand, no doubt ready to make a bunch of calls, Lily grinned at me. "We did it, Sara. Thank you so much. You're the best friend ever, in the history of the world."

And that was pretty much the best thing to hear, ever, in the history of the world.

Chapter 15

When I got home a short time later, I found Lady Azura up early—for her—and bustling around her séance room. She was setting out stones. They looked like ruby crystals.

"Ah, there you are, Sara," she said, her tone brusque as if she meant business. "Do you still have that ruby crystal I gave you last summer?"

This startled me. Was she going to talk to me about my love life?

"Yes," I replied warily. "Why do you ask?"

"Have you noticed that it's been more active recently?"

I nodded. "It's been vibrating, like, nonstop. And sometimes I feel it heat up. What's going on?"

As if to answer, the ruby crystals on the table all trembled noticeably, as though they were in an earthquake or something. Lady Azura looked at me and nodded.

"The ruby crystal is a very special gemstone. As you know, it has properties that can help to make love bloom, but it has even greater powers than that. It is also the gemstone that represents the sun. A solar event is coming, Sara. The ruby crystals are vibrating because of the impending solar event."

"A solar event?" I had no idea what she was talking about.

"Yes. Do you remember when I told you that I was picking up on atmospheric disturbances? Well, this is what I was sensing." Lady Azura spoke quickly, and I could tell she was really excited. "Solar flare activity has been steadily increasing for the past few weeks. Ever since the hurricane. I have learned that it is about to reach its highest point in almost thirty years. So now is an excellent time to think about your wish."

Ordinarily I would have asked Lady Azura how she had learned this—she wasn't exactly one to surf the web—but I was too distracted by her mention of a wish.

"My wish?" I repeated.

"Yes, Sara. You need to think long and hard about what your deepest wish is and put it out there into the universe. Wishes made during the time of peak solar flare episodes will come true if they are destined to be so. This is a marvelous opportunity. Very exciting."

She picked up a ruby crystal from the table and wrapped it in her palm and held it close to her heart. "This is especially true for you, because your chart is so heavily influenced by the sun. I believe the peak is supposed to be tomorrow sometime. So you must meditate today to decide what your wish is. Do you understand what I am telling you?"

Something clicked in my mind.

"Was my mom's chart also ruled by the sun?"

Lady Azura looked at me curiously, and then nodded. "Yes, it was, in fact. Why do you ask?"

"Um, I can't explain right now. But Lady Azura, thank you for telling me this. I promise I will talk about it more with you later, but right now I have to go do something. Is that okay?"

It wasn't something I usually did—ask her permission to leave her room. But I didn't want to just leave her hanging. I needed for her to know that I knew this was important.

She knew.

"Go ahead, Sara," she told me, a smile playing on her crimson lips.

I nodded and headed upstairs to my room. Closed the door. Logged on to my computer and researched solar flares in my area. What I found confirmed what I had already figured out.

There was a lot of solar activity in the fall of 1984. An unusually large amount of activity. Just at the time when my mother was keeping her journal.

My mother's powers must have been heightened by the solar flares. The same way my own powers seemed to have been heightened recently. I had never before had so many visions. I believed it was the solar activity that was causing me to be able to have all those visions about my mom. And the way I had just known that the spirits I was seeing were somehow related to Lily's dad's land deal . . . that was definitely out of the ordinary. I was sure the solar activity had made my intuition stronger.

And there was more, I realized as I sat on the floor

of my room, my thoughts tumbling around in my mind. My mom's wish to get rid of her powers must have coincided with the peak of the solar flare. She made it almost without thinking, not knowing that an environmental phenomenon she had probably never even heard of was going to make her wish come true. There was no way to know that for sure, but I felt it was true deep down and in my heart.

That was all the proof I needed.

I suddenly felt a new bond with my mother. We were experiencing almost the exact same solar event, thirty years apart. But unlike my mother, I could make my solar flare wish knowing the power it held. I would be able to choose my wish wisely.

I decided not to cancel my date with Mason. But I also decided to make it happen on my terms, rather than his. I texted him and asked him to meet me at Scoops at seven.

He didn't sound that happy about the change in location. But I was pretty firm. And then he agreed.

He was waiting for me when I got there. He'd chosen a small booth as far from the door as you could get.

Almost like he didn't want to be seen together. Again.

I said hi and slid into the seat across from him. I think he must have sensed a change in my attitude. He held the huge, laminated menu up in front of him like a shield. Which was funny, because no one ever looked at the menu at Scoops. The ice-cream flavors were all posted behind the counter, and the toppings were all on the tables.

"What do you want?" I asked, standing up. "My treat tonight." I still had fifteen dollars left over from the money my dad had given me for the arcade the previous Sunday.

"Uh, chocolate milk shake," he replied. "Are you sure? I mean, I was going to treat."

"Yep, I got it," I said.

I returned a few minutes later, putting his milk shake down in front of him and then sliding in with my sundae. We slurped and spooned in awkward silence for a few moments. Then I spoke up.

"So I almost canceled," I said.

He set down his milk shake. Swallowed. Raised his eyebrows in question.

"Yeah. It's kind of been bothering me about how

uncomfortable it seems to make you for us to be seen together."

He shrugged and became deeply engrossed in studying his spoon. I waited for him to say something. Finally he did.

"I guess I'm just not ready to be so out there with . . . you know," he mumbled.

"With what? Our mutual powers?"

Nod.

"Well, I'm pretty comfortable with mine," I said. "I'm really glad I have them. I guess I can understand if you're not comfortable with your own, um, situation, but I feel like you're not comfortable with mine, either. My powers. With who I am, I mean."

I was rambling a little bit, but I knew I had made my point.

"Listen," he said, setting down the spoon and looking me straight in the eye. "I think it's cool how strong you are. But I just don't want to deal with all this stuff with powers right now. It's been weird enough, being at a new school with all these new kids, right after telling my parents about . . . everything I can do. It's just a lot to deal with, and I'm sick of it."

"But that's just it, Mason. You kind of have to deal with it. Do you see that?"

Several napkins flew out of the dispenser on our table, twirled around a few times in the air, and then landed gently on the table in front of us. Mason's face turned red, and I saw him glance around, checking to see if anyone had noticed.

I didn't check. I didn't really care if anyone had seen it. But that was the difference between us.

"You know what I think?" I said slowly. "I think maybe it would be better if we didn't go out right now. Maybe when you're more comfortable with your powers, who you are, we can start hanging out again. But for right now, it doesn't seem like we're a great match together."

I had a weird out-of-body moment. I heard the words coming out of my mouth like I was standing next to myself, listening. I was amazed to be hearing myself saying them. I would never have had the confidence to say something like this to a boy even a few months ago.

Mason nodded. "I guess you're right," he said. "But for the record? I think you're a pretty cool girl."

I smiled. "Thanks, Mason," I said. "I think you're pretty cool too."

Chapter 16

I headed straight to Lily's the next morning, Sunday.

She hugged me when she saw me, and then pulled me inside and closed the door. "So much to tell you," she said. "Let's go to my room."

"I have so much to tell *you*," I said, brimming with happiness that I had such a wonderful best friend. I followed her upstairs.

Once we were in her room with the door closed, Lily gave me another huge bear hug. "Everything is going to be totally fine!" she squealed in excitement. "My dad's lawyer talked to the seller's lawyer, and even though they've already signed the contract, they agreed to split the cost of excavating those old, crumbly pipes. And then because half the town's zoning commission is related to us, my dad told me he's ninety percent sure the town is going to help out with the cost too! And a reporter from the *New York Times* called us! They're sending a reporter out to do a story on the cave-in and everything!"

"That's such amazing news, Lil," I said, taking her hand and squeezing it. Then I told her about Mason, and how I kind of, sort of broke up with him, but that I wasn't feeling terrible and didn't think he was either. "I feel really mature," I said. "Instead of running away, I talked it all over with him, told him just how I felt. I don't think either of us is going to, like, hide when we see each other."

"I'm really proud of you," said Lily, her dark eyes sparkling. "I kind of, sort of broke up with Cal last night too. I was just so sick of doing all the talking when we got together. I mean, I know I'm talkative and he's, well, boring, so that shouldn't surprise me, but I think I'm better off with someone who has a personality. Any personality! I'm not *that* picky. Even though he is quite good-looking."

She'd spoken so fast, without taking a breath, that she'd kind of run out of oxygen by the time she got to the end of her speech. Which made us both crack up.

But then her brow furrowed.

"What's the matter?" I asked her.

She flopped down into her chair. "I just feel like you've been bothered by something recently, and I suspect it's the diary, because you haven't once mentioned it, even though I've delicately tried to bring it up with you." Her words tumbled out rapidly again. "And even though it's none of my business, I feel like I should be helping you deal with whatever it is that's bothering you. But I don't want to pry or anything."

I sat down on the bed across from her chair, so our knees were almost touching. I smiled gratefully at her. "You're right. I have been kind of bothered by it."

I told her about what I'd read in my mom's diary. About how ashamed I'd been feeling because of the way she had treated Lady Azura. How confused I was that she didn't want powers, and that she spent so much of her time wishing them away. How desperately she seemed to want to conform socially. "It's just really hard to think this about my mom, who I've wanted to meet my whole life. Now, when I come as close as I'll probably ever get to meeting her, I don't really like what I see." I felt a huge lump rise in my throat. It was really hard to swallow. "I couldn't even get all the way through the diary. I just shoved it on a shelf in my closet. I'm not sure I'll ever finish it now."

Lily stood up from the chair and sat down next to me on the bed, so we were sitting shoulder to shoulder. "You know, Sar, I also keep a journal."

"You do?" I managed to swallow down the lump so my voice came out more or less normal. "I've been trying too. But I decided to do it through photos, since I'm more about visuals. You're such an awesome writer. It's probably a great journal."

"Yeah, well, no. Not really. Most of it is really dumb. But I write in it almost every day. I've been doing it since sixth grade. And let me tell you something. When I go back and read some of the stuff I wrote, even just last year, I usually cringe at the person I was. So much of the stuff I once thought was a crisis seems so unimportant now. So immature. But then I remind myself that a journal is just like a snapshot in time. It's a picture of a person on a given day, at a certain time of her life, captured on a page. That's the same with your mother's diary, I'm sure. If she had read later the stuff you're reading now, she would also probably think it's immature and unimportant. I wouldn't be too hard on her."

As Lily talked, I thought about what my journal might read like today, if I had written one a year ago or two years ago. Would there be some seriously cringe-inducing material in there?

Absolutely.

"People use diaries and journals for all kinds of things," Lily went on. "To vent. To say stuff they'd never say to anyone else. We don't get to go back and rewrite them."

"That all makes sense," I said. "But why did my mother seem to want me to find the journal? If she wasn't proud of what was in it, then why did she go to so much trouble to send me the message through Duggan?"

Lily shrugged. "Not sure. But that's why you need to finish reading it."

It was such a simple answer, but one I had not thought of myself.

Lily was right, as usual.

I promised Lily I would finish it. And that I would report back to her about what I'd learned. I also told her I was getting ready to tell my dad and Lady Azura about it. But that first I was going to read it to the end, just by myself.

I went home. Headed straight upstairs to my room. Took the diary out from where I'd stashed it behind my old boots. Then I sat down on the floor next to my bed to read it. Again.

I picked up where I'd left off. I read page after page of a twelve-year-old girl's thoughts and fears and insecurities. It progressed through the winter and continued into the spring of her seventh-grade year. There was no more about having powers. By April, there were just sporadic entries, spaced a week, ten days, three days, then a whole month apart. My mom seemed to be losing interest in the diary a little. There was stuff about clothes. Boys she liked. A new camera her mother had bought her. How her photography teacher had told her he thought she had a lot of talent. That made me smile.

And then the journal seemed to end. There were about fifty remaining pages, left blank, after the last entry, dated May 12, 1985, where she mentioned that her mom had bought a house in Connecticut, and that they'd have to start packing the second school was out, and would move there sometime in late June.

I was about to set the book down when I noticed a page with writing on it. It was a final entry at the back of the book, a few pages from the end. The writing covered several pages. It was dated November 1988.

That meant my mom was sixteen when she wrote it.

Three and a half years had gone by between the last entry of the diary and this final one.

My breath caught in my throat as I began reading what my mother had written there. It was a letter.

A letter to me.

Chapter 17

Dear Sara,

You don't know me yet, but I'm your mother. Gosh, that was a weird sentence to write.

I'm only sixteen, so I am technically not your mother yet, but I will be someday. I haven't even met the guy I'm going to marry yet. I don't know when that's going to happen. I kind of hope it doesn't happen too soon, because the first thing I want to do is go to college, and then graduate, and become a world-famous photographer. So I don't even know what your last name will be. But I feel pretty sure that after I do grow up and do all these things and then get married, I'm going to have a baby and she will be you. And your name is going to be Sara. I feel sure because you told me it would happen.

I know this is hard to understand, but last night you

came to visit me in a dream. It was a dream unlike any I've ever had. It was definitely a dream—I was asleep when it happened—but it's like it really happened in real life and not just in a dream. Does that make any sense at all?

I'm staying at my grandmother—your future great-grandmother—Lady Azura's house. That might explain a lot, because whenever strange things have happened to me in my life, they've happened when I was around my grandmother.

My mom and Lady Azura have patched things up. If you've read the beginning of this diary (cringe—some of it is really dumb, sorry), you will know that they had a big fight. The summer after my year at Stellamar, we moved to Connecticut. That was almost four years ago. Now they get along okay. They are really different from each other. But deep down, they do have a lot in common. Hopefully by the time you're reading this, you will know both of them well, so you'll know what I mean.

My eyes teared up as I realized that my mom would have had no way of knowing, at sixteen, that her own mother was going to die so young. That I would never get to meet her, either.

I closed the book. Sat there with it on my lap for a really long time with tears rolling down my cheeks.

Once when I was about four years old, I fell off our play set in the backyard. I landed flat on my back. For several seconds, I couldn't breathe. Couldn't cry out. Couldn't feel pain. I guess it's called getting the wind knocked out of you. I just lay there, staring up at the blue sky. I remember it so vividly. I could hear the leaves rustling on the trees.

And then my dad came barreling out of the house. He'd been watching me from the window, I guess, and saw what happened. He scooped me up and suddenly I could breathe again, and talk, and I cried even though I wasn't really hurt. Just shocked.

That was the way I felt now.

But slowly, I felt a warmth spread over me. It started in my chest, and then spread steadily outward, until I felt it warming my fingers and toes and the top of my head. It was an amazing feeling. It was love. Love for my mother, who had written me this letter. Given me this gift.

I couldn't wait to make my wish on the solar

flare. I knew it was going to come true. Maybe not today, and maybe not tomorrow, but someday it would come true.

My wish was to meet my mother's spirit.

SARANORMAL

Every spirit.

Every secret.

Every moment from the beginning.

About the Author

Phoebe Rivers had a brush with the paranormal when she was thirteen years old, and ever since then she has been fascinated by people who see spirits and can communicate with them. In addition to her intrigue with all things paranormal, Phoebe also loves cats, French cuisine, and writing stories. She has written dozens of books for children of all ages and is thrilled to now be exploring Sara's paranormal world.